HOOP CITY

DETROIT

SAM MOUSSAVI

EPIC
Press

Detroit
Hoop City: Book #2

Written by Sam Moussavi

Copyright © 2016 by Abdo Consulting Group, Inc.

Published by EPIC Press™
PO Box 398166
Minneapolis, MN 55439

Cover design by Nicole Ramsay
Images for cover art obtained from Shutterstock.com
Edited by Lisa Owens

LIBRARY OF CONGRESS CATALOGING-IN-PUBLICATION DATA

Moussavi, Sam.
Detroit / Sam Moussavi.
p. cm. — (Hoop city)
Summary: Isaiah is a hot-shot freshman, talented and hard-working enough to be
on the varsity basketball team at one of the top private high schools in Detroit. Will
he be able to rise above the taunts from teammates and opponents, while trying to
overcome the deconstruction of his family?
ISBN 978-1-68076-045-3 (hardcover)
1. Basketball—Fiction. 2. High schools—Fiction. 3. Inner cities—Fiction.
4. Teamwork—Fiction. 5. Young adult fiction. I. Title.
[Fic]—dc23
2015903975

EPICPRESS.COM

*To Marina, with a white butterfly fluttering
just above her shoulder*

ONE

I was just a freshman during the year that my life completely changed. I didn't know anything about the world, but that didn't bother me because I figured I had time. Both of my parents were still in the picture—they were still technically together then.

I was a lucky one and not just because I had both parents. My luck extended to where I lived compared to where all of the rest of my teammates did. I lived in Auburn Hills, Michigan. Most people only know it as the home of the Detroit Pistons, but to me, Auburn Hills was the only place I ever called home.

Most of my teammates lived in Detroit proper. After practice, when they rode the bus or walked to their small apartments, I got into a black Mercedes with my dad and onto the 75 north highway toward our five bedroom house in Auburn Hills. And on that thirty-something mile trip home from the city, I would think about how great it would be to live in Detroit. I would think about all those tall buildings in front of gray skies. And finally, I would think about basketball, and how sweet it would be to show them that I was not only good enough, but tough enough, too.

It didn't matter that I had never lived there before. And it didn't matter that I had not "lived hard." All my life was spent playing basketball and going to school in Detroit. It was all I knew. In my mind, it only made sense to live there as well.

"Why can't we move into the city?" I said to my dad, one cloudy day after school in late September, on the drive back to Auburn Hills. Detroit was famous for its cloudy days.

He looked at me like I was crazy.

"Ask any of your teammates if they would switch places with you," he said. "I bet you'd have ten niggas piled up in this Mercedes, while your narrow ass is sittin' there freezing on the corner of Vernor and Junction."

He laughed at the thought. After a few more seconds of driving, we both did.

It was rare for my dad to crack a joke or even to smile. And when he did, I made sure to smile too, because those moments were few and far between.

My dad was a serious man. He was an ex-player who made his way out of the projects in Boston to a scholarship at Providence University in Rhode Island. He made it all the way to being drafted in the second round by the Detroit Pistons. He played in the NBA for six years, bouncing around to a few other teams after Detroit, and played another five in the European leagues. He came home from Europe and called it a career after eleven years of being a pro athlete.

The day after he was drafted to the NBA, he married my mother, and the day after he signed his first pro contract, he bought his first house in Auburn Hills. Growing up in the projects, there was never a place that he could call home. When he was able to make it happen financially, he made sure that he and *his* had a place to settle—that we had a place to call home.

Auburn Hills was that place.

Even when he was traded to other NBA teams, and later, when he went to Europe, my mom and I stayed behind in Auburn Hills. He didn't want to drag us all over the world while he chased his dream of playing pro ball. He wanted the roots that he laid down in Auburn Hills to grow and remain strong.

"Why haven't I ever played for a school in Auburn Hills?" I said. "I mean, why have I only gone to schools in Detroit when there are perfectly good schools close to where we live?"

We were almost home, Detroit long in the rear

view. The car was quiet before I spoke. My dad never said anything when there wasn't anything to say.

He smiled. "You have a scholarship to play ball at one of the best prep schools in all of the country, Isaiah," he said, as he kept his eyes on the road. "Not just in this part of the country. The *entire* country."

I didn't say anything.

"Do you really need me to answer *that* question?" he said, looking over to me.

"They call me 'soft,'" I said. "Some of the other guys on the team. They don't think I'm tough enough, because I grew up in the burbs."

"Well, you do have that going against you," he said, with a smirk that was meant to sting a little.

"One of the guys said that I ain't black enough."

"Why, 'cause you didn't grow up in the city? That's just stupid."

I nodded.

"Ignore it," he said. "They already know you can

ball. You just gotta show them that you're tough. And growing up in the projects doesn't make you tough, believe me."

I stared at him, waiting for him to talk some more.

"You'll be fine," he said.

More silence.

Ignoring the taunts was easier said than done. I appreciated my dad's advice. Always. I knew he loved me and wanted the best for me. But I also knew that things weren't going to go as smoothly as he said they would.

"Dad," I said, "is this a big year for me? It feels like a big year."

He cracked another smile. Two in one day. That was a rare feat. I can't even remember the last time he smiled during a car ride home from the city. He was usually on his cell, or just staring straight ahead.

"Son," he said, "you're black. They're all big."

And with that we pulled into the driveway of

our three-story house in Auburn Hills. The one my dad—another nigga from the projects—owned outright. He took pride in that fact and usually when we pulled up to it, he looked at it as if he were laying eyes on it for the first time. Owning properties in the suburbs—as well as in Detroit— wasn't a big deal to my dad because he owned many of them through his real estate company, formed after his playing days. It went like this: he bought up as many old houses as he could, fixed them up, and then flipped them for profit. Other than lessons on basketball, he'd always preach to me about buying real estate when I got older. "Buy land, Isaiah," he would say, "'cause God ain't makin' any more of it." Still, our house was more than just land. It was special to him. It was the first one he ever owned and it was the only house I had ever lived in. It was the place where we became a family.

Something had changed though. My dad barely looked up at the house that day and I realized this was happening more and more. He didn't take his keys out of the ignition and get out of the car. He didn't say anything, just waited for me to get out.

"Isaiah," he said, after rolling the passenger's window down and leaning over.

"Yeah, Dad?"

"I'll be back in an hour or two," he said. "Last workout before the season starts."

I nodded and then he left. He still "lived" at the house but hadn't slept there in the past six months. Our house was just a storage place for his basketball memorabilia these days. He'd been stayin' someplace else at nights. We didn't know where. I wasn't brave enough to ask. Still, he never failed to let me or my mom know that: "I can set foot in this house anytime I damn please. I paid for it."

The house looked quiet and empty from outside. I stood there in front of it, staring, wishing that things would change.

I knew there was a problem. But I didn't say anything. I didn't know what to say.

The sun was shining in Auburn Hills even though Detroit was covered by a big, gray cloud.

TWO

"Mom," I said in a low voice. Not quite a whisper, but barely above one. It didn't feel right waking her up. But it also didn't feel right that she'd be fast asleep in the afternoon. I nudged her a little.

She snored loudly and turned over on her other side, away from me. It was no use getting her up at that point. I stared at her back for a couple of seconds.

I left her room, closing the door softly, and went to the kitchen to look for something to eat. There was nothing on the stove, nothing in the oven. My mom stopped cooking when my dad stopped living there. There was frozen food in the freezer and salty snacks in the pantry, but I didn't want to eat any of it. I had a banana and bowl of cereal.

I still had a couple hours before my dad would be back to pick me up for the workout. My first season of varsity basketball was right around corner, with the opening practice the next day after school. But in my dad's eyes, there was still time to sneak in one more tough workout.

Whenever I wasn't in season—meaning the summer and fall—he would put me through a series of demanding workouts. During summertime when there was no school, we'd start at seven in the morning with weights, conditioning, and on-court fundamentals, before taking a break for lunch and recovery. We followed that up with another evening workout that focused on shooting, and ended with pick-up games against guys who were older than me. All of these workouts happened in Detroit. Never in Auburn Hills. All of the guys I played against were either friends of my dad's or college players from the city that he knew. He didn't want me playing on a team like most of my teammates did. He wanted to control who I played against and who I associated with. When I was in school, the workout schedule was the same, except I had to be out of bed by four-thirty in the morning instead of seven. I'd have these workouts at least four times a week when I wasn't in season. I was relieved that the season was close. Just one more tough workout before I could just focus on playing. I loved playing in games. I hated the training part, but knew it was important. My dad helped me recognize that.

He also expected me to have all my homework done. I complained all the time that it was impossible to do well in school and work out this hard. His only reply was a shoulder shrug.

I took a bite of my cereal and flipped open my math homework. I stared at it for a while, wondering just how I could get it all done. I really wanted to do what my mother was doing. I wanted to flop down on the couch, turn on the TV, and not worry about training or quadratic equations or my dad's hard stare.

There wasn't enough time in my life time to be Isaiah. Not Isaiah the basketball player—just Isaiah the kid. My dad wouldn't allow it. He made that much clear. His house, his rules.

THREE

My dad pulled the Mercedes up to the driveway two hours later like clockwork. I ran out of the house and got in. The air was crisp and it smelled like snow was coming. We headed back to Detroit—back to the gym that we had always gone to in the northeastern part of town.

I started playing basketball at the age of five and by the time I turned ten, my dad started helping me work on my game. When he saw that I *had* a little game, the heavy workouts started. I was about twelve. That's also when we started playing one-on-one at the end of every workout. He went easy on me at first, and then he stopped. According to him, twelve years old was the age that I would begin to figure out what kind of man I was going to be. I guess part of my figuring that out was getting my ass kicked around the gym.

The gym doubled as a boxing center and there were always rumors flying around that my dad owned a piece of it. The rumors were probably true because we could use it at any time, day or night. He was famous there and that made me kind of famous too. People looked up to him—to us. When we hit the floor for a game of one-on-one, people would gather to watch us go at it. One of our battles reached the point of legend because it was on Thanksgiving, of all nights. I was only thirteen for that game. And he barely beat me, eleven to nine. That was the closest I ever came to beating him one-on-one.

Once again, he didn't say much on the ride to the gym. He cleared his throat when I told him that my mother was asleep when I got home from school.

When we got to the gym, there were a few guys outside smoking cigarettes. My dad slowed the car, rolled the window down and glared at them. A cold rush of air flooded the car. The guys scattered like roaches down to the other end of the block.

"Motherfuckers," he said.

We parked behind the gym, in the same spot we always parked in.

Inside were all the sounds you'd expect from a gym. You could hear fists colliding with speed bags, you could hear old men shouting behind heavy bags, and you could also hear dumbbells clanging. All of this noise was on top of the soul music in the background, the music my dad called "Motown."

"Go get changed," he said. "I gotta talk to Mr. Jones."

I nodded and went into the locker room.

Ten minutes later, I was changed and ready to go. I hit the floor and started to stretch alongside my dad.

"What's up with Mr. Jones?"

"Don't worry about it," he said. "You need to worry about that weak-ass right hand you got."

"Yeah, whatever."

"I'm serious," he said, as he stretched his long left arm over his right side. My dad was in great shape. And this wasn't considering his age and the fact that he played pro ball until the age of thirty-three. He was in good shape no matter which way you cut it.

Most of his old friends from the Pistons had bald heads and big guts, but not him. Every grueling workout I went through, he did too. And that made it easier for me. Knowing that someone else was going through the same thing I was going through. My dad used to say that that's what playing on a pro team was like. You scrap, claw, and bleed to get to a place that most people can't even dream of. And once you get there, you do the exact same things to get wins. You do those things together. When my legs used to burn and my body felt like it was on the edge of exhaustion, I could lean on another person to give me strength and energy. That person just happened to be my dad.

Stretching was through and then my dad got his favorite ball—with the perfect grip—out of his gym bag. That was the only ball we ever used during our workouts. He passed it to me.

"All right," he said. "Let's get better. And let's see if you can finally beat me."

As always, we started with on-court work: dribbling, footwork, and then shooting. Next, we did drills that called for getting up and down the court. This was my second favorite part of our workouts, because it focused on my speed. I ran back and forth, up and down, stopping on a dime and pulling up for jumpers. By the time that drill was over, I needed a rest to give my wobbly legs a chance to recover.

After that, the only thing left was the one-on-one game. My favorite part.

"Ready to get your ass kicked?" he said, with a

smirk that held both a joking tone and a serious one at the same time.

"Tonight's the night," I said. "Time for me to—"

"Quit talking," he said, as he tossed the ball at my chest.

I always got the ball first because I was always the loser from the game before. We played to eleven, all ones, but you had to win by two. You make it, you take it. And you had to clear everything, even air balls.

I jumped out on him three to zero. But this was nothing new. I had a lot of leads on him in our games over the years, but I faded at the end. He quickly evened the score and then some, with five points of his own. After he missed his next shot, I grabbed the rebound, took it back to clear it, and then canned a step-back jumper right in his face.

"Nice," he said, like a robot, not looking me in the eye.

Even after all those years of playing professionally,

he was focused on beating me. He tried to teach me to have the same kind of focus he did, but I wasn't so sure that it was something I could learn. I felt like I was picking it up a little, though there were still times where my mind would slip to my mom or school; I think that's why he would always beat me. His mind never slipped. Win. Compete. That was all he knew.

The score was tied at nine and I had possession of the ball. I had it in my left hand and gave him a quick in-and-out dribble. He fell off balance and a small crease to the basket opened. I took it and as I felt him closing in from behind for the block, I flipped the ball high off the glass with my left hand. In his attempt to contest, he slammed into me and we both took a spill underneath the basket.

I didn't see if the shot went in because I was on the floor, underneath my dad. He helped me up.

"That's what I'm talking about," he said. "Concentration. That was a really nice move. You anticipated me. Your mind was ahead of mine."

I was up ten to nine with a chance to end the game. The rule was you had to win by two, so beating him eleven to nine would work. I had been this close to beating him many times, only to fail in some crucial way at the end. Something felt different this time. I was confident that I could take him.

I checked the ball to him and he fired it back to me. He crouched down into his defensive stance, eyeing me the entire time. He was trying to intimidate me, not only to make me stronger, but also because deep down inside, he still hated to lose. I could see it in his eyes.

I looked straight back into his eyes. I was ready to take him.

I dribbled the ball carefully, protecting it against his constant, heavy swipes. It wasn't easy to shake him when he was this locked in. The swell of confidence I had from just seconds before wavered. With every timid dribble, he got stronger and more imposing. I pulled the ball back out of the key to reset, taking a deep breath in the process. I wanted to get a running start at him. His feet stopped for a split second and I attacked to the left, my strong side. I got half a step on him, but he quickly recovered and cut me off. He swiped at the ball again, missing it by an inch, chopping down on my left arm instead. That left him exposed and overextended. In an instant, I attacked again to the left. When he tried to catch up, I crossed it back over to the right and lost him. His shoes squeaked for mercy on the hardwood. Mine stopped on a dime. His ankles gave out. He lost his balance. The only thing that stopped him from falling down was the free hand he used to prop himself up like a kickstand. I had put him on skates, and on his way down, his eyes met mine. I rose up for a jumper that felt good—more than good—coming off my hand. I followed the arc of the ball with my eyes. He turned his head and did the same. It swished through the net and whipped against the air, creating that perfect sound. The perfect sound to any basketball player.

Swish. My win. My time.

I didn't know how to react because I had never beaten him before. I don't think he knew how to react. This was new to both of us.

He grabbed the ball and squeezed it tight with both hands. He bounced it off the floor—hard—two times. Each dribble brought a thump and then an echo into the empty gym. He walked over, stood right in front of me, and glared down. The thrill of the win added courage to my stance and I met his gaze. He came in close, touched his forehead to mine, and then finally, patted me on the head. "Good game," he said.

He handed me the ball and I accepted it.

It felt good to finally beat him. The pat on the head felt even better.

We walked out of the gym and he threw an arm around my shoulder.

FOUR

It was freezing outside by the time I got into the car. My dad pulled it around to the front as he waited for Mr. Jones to lock up. I cranked up the heat to high as they talked underneath a dim street light.

There were three men in front of a vacant house across the street. Two of them stood on the sidewalk looking over at Mr. Jones and my dad, while the third one was closer to the vacant house. After a few seconds, he pulled the board—in place of a front door—clean off the house. He went inside and the other two looked across the street again before following. They replaced the board from inside and then the street was silent, other than the low voices of Mr. Jones and my dad. It was strange to see *those* men sneaking into a vacant. They didn't look homeless. They really didn't even look poor, as their clothes were not dirty or torn.

When the two men in front of the gym finished talking, they shook hands. My dad blew into a fist and rubbed his hands together as he got into the car. He pulled it away from the gym.

"You did a good job tonight, Isaiah," he said, as we drove onto Grand Boulevard. There were more vacants here—a lot of them, because Grand was a main road. And like they had been for a long time, times were tough in Detroit.

"And it's good," he said. "Because people are going to try you out there on the court. They gonna test you."

I nodded blankly, focusing more on the empty houses rushing by. I wondered how many people there would be if the boards were peeled back on all of them.

"Boy! What are you lookin' at out there? See this is what I'm talking about! Focus that brain."

"Sorry."

"Shit. You all over the place," he said.

My heart beat a little faster when I replied, "Well, I beat you tonight, didn't I?"

Dad ignored this comment. "What did you eat when you got home from school?" he asked.

I didn't answer him because I didn't want him to badmouth my mom.

He shook his head. "She needs to pick her lazy ass up and cook you a meal. She has that whole big house to herself and all she uses is that damn bed!"

"She doesn't sleep all the time, Dad. And besides, I'm fine. I can feed myself. I can take care of myself."

"Oh, you can?"

"Yeah," I said.

"Your little fourteen-year-old ass ain't close to being ready to be a man," he laughed.

He was probably right. My feelings weren't hurt,

though. I was just happy to see him laughing. The truth is, I wasn't really sure if I could take care of myself.

"I'll get someone over to the house." He put his eyes back on the road. "To cook your meals during the season."

"Mom can do it," I said.

He shook his head again.

"Playing varsity as a freshman will be a challenge. With all the hype you're coming in with, there's gonna be some jealousy and things like that. It's gonna be just you out there at the beginning."

"I'll show them I can play."

"You gotta be sharp at all moments, both mentally and physically. It ain't all about what you do on the court, either."

He didn't look at me when he said this. He stayed focused on the road.

"You saying that you can take care of yourself—that's the right attitude," he said. "It's a good start. But the truth is that you're gonna need help."

I listened, but only partially. My eyes crept back to the streets and the rows and rows of vacants. Everything around us looked cold, black, and lonely. The sky was black too. It was like this until we took the lighted highway ramp for the 75 north.

"You're ready, though," he said, after a period of silence. "You can handle it."

I continued staring out the window. Even though my eyes only saw trees, my mind stayed with the vacants.

By the time we got back to Auburn Hills, it was late and I was wiped. I wasn't sure if my mom would be awake and was too tired to worry about it.

When we pulled up to the house, there were no lights on.

"You coming in?" I said.

He looked at the house, then at me. "Nah. I'll pick you up before school tomorrow."

"Okay."

I got out of the car.

He called my name before I shut the door and I ducked my head back in.

He put a fist out for a dap. "I'm proud of you, Isaiah."

I pounded it. "Thanks."

"I love you, son."

"Love you too, Dad."

FIVE

"You are too short."

That's what I heard growing up. Over and over. From opposing players, from some coaches who didn't know anything about my desire to be great. Even my dad would say it to get under my skin.

I never listened to any of it from anybody. What I lacked in height I made up for with speed and relentlessness. While I was out on the floor, I went as hard as I could, for as long as I could. And that's what separated me from everyone else.

It landed me a scholarship to one of the most the prestigious Catholic high schools in Detroit.

Detroit Catholic's athletic tradition was rich; the basketball program produced college players—too many to count—and even a few pros over the years. I accepted their offer for two reasons: first, I wanted to be a part of the tradition. Second, and more important to me, the school was in a tough part of Detroit. I wanted to be a part of the city.

For as long I could remember, basketball was my mission in life. My dad had a lot to do with that, for obvious reasons. But he never pushed me to play. It was just part of me—in my blood.

I was going to play varsity from the start, as only the second freshman in school history to do so. Coach said that he planned to bring me along slowly and that I had to earn a spot in the starting lineup. But I didn't worry about any of that. I knew I was going to be a big part of the team because of how hard I worked. It wouldn't take me long to crack the starting five.

Our team was not expected to be as strong as it was the year before, when they had a veteran team with seven seniors. That team won the city championship. I watched a lot of their games that year as I was getting to know the school. The team relied on those seniors, with only one junior contributing in a meaningful way. That junior, now a senior, was named Sherrod Swope. He was expected—at least, until I hit my stride—to be the best player on the team as well as the only proven leader. Sherrod played the two and I couldn't wait to take the starting point guard position and play right next to him. With a team full of young players, Coach made it clear that you didn't have to be an upperclassmen to be a leader. After getting a starting a spot, becoming a leader on the team would be my second goal.

It was time for the first practice of the season. I was anxious to get started. Even though I didn't play summer league, I knew all of the guys on the team from visits to the school the year before.

"What up, rookie?" Dorrell said as he passed by. He played on the team the season before and he would be my main competition for the starting point guard spot.

"Sup," I nodded.

He eyed me as he talked to another player who played on the team the year before. He smirked before turning his back and walking to the other end of the court.

I knew it would be hard at first. But I wasn't there to make friends. I was there to compete.

Sherrod and I were closer because we worked out together in the summer. He also didn't play on the school's summer league team, instead playing AAU on a travel team from the city. My dad was a mentor to Sherrod going back to when he was a sophomore. And that's when he started coming over to our gym to work out. He was only able to make it to five workouts that summer because of AAU tournaments. But those five workouts were intense. We even went at it during one pick-up game. Sherrod is a tough kid from the city and I knew that I'd have to prove myself to him because of the zip code I grew up in. In the end, I think that surprised him. After that, I just knew we were going to be the two best players on the team in the winter.

Sherrod walked into the gym confidently before practice and came straight over to me. You could tell he was the leader of the pack just by the way he carried himself. We dapped up. I was respectful to him when we first met during the summer. I didn't want him thinking that I was cocky with no skill and work ethic to back it up. But I also wanted to compete with him and not back down. I knew that would be the only way to gain his respect.

I stood next to him before the first practice of the season as an equal. And it was all because of those summer workouts.

"You ready to get *this* going?" he said.

"Yeah," I said. "I'm about to explode. Workouts are over and it's time for business."

He nodded and walked over to the trainer to get stretched out.

Even though I never lacked confidence, my growing friendship with Sherrod gave me even more. He saw how hard I worked and knew that he could trust me. Unfortunately, the other guys on the team didn't get a chance to see that yet. I would show them shortly.

———

Practice was easy. I was the fastest player on the court. And in terms of being in shape, that was a tie between me and Sherrod. No surprise there. The workouts paid off right there on the first day of practice. I got stronger as the practice wore on. While everyone else, other than Sherrod, was the opposite.

Sherrod had a good first practice as well. He made the game look so easy. He knew the offense inside and out and put all the other guys in their proper positions out on the floor. During the short scrimmage at the end of practice, Coach put me on the other team so I could guard Sherrod. I held my own just like during the summer. Although he scored eleven points and dished out three assists, I answered with ten points, plus four assists. I also had no turnovers when he guarded me and one steal from him.

Playing against him made me a better player and that was exciting because we had the whole season to go at each other in practice. I actually felt bad for the teams on our schedule. They weren't going to be able to deal with a backcourt of Sherrod and me.

After Coach's post-practice talk, he asked me to break the huddle. I accepted, and everyone put their hand in the middle before I called out, "Champs on three! Champs on three! One, two, three!"

"Champs!"

Dorrell bumped into to me on purpose after we broke the huddle. He saw me as a threat to his position. And he wasn't wrong about that. I would've been worried too if I were him. What bothered me was that he thought I was soft. He thought he could just bump me and I would take it.

"What was that all about?" I said.

"You a fake ass nigga, you know that?" Dorrell said, looking me up and down.

"What?"

"You heard me," he said. "You not even from Detroit. Need to get your ass back over to Auburn Hills 'fore shit gets real."

"Whatever."

"Yeah, we'll see," he said.

He walked off the floor toward the locker room. I didn't care about his threats. That wasn't going to stop me from taking his spot in the starting five. But it did get on my nerves that he questioned my toughness.

Someone called my name from behind. It was a familiar voice. I turned around and saw my dad. He walked over and we slapped five.

"How do you feel?" he said.

"I feel good."

"What was that all about after practice?"

"Dorrell?"

He nodded.

"He's just mad because I'm about to be the starting point guard. If not today, then definitely tomorrow."

He smiled and so did I.

"Sherrod is good," I said.

"He is," he said. "You looked fast out there."

"I felt fast."

"The thing with Dorrell?" he said. "You got it, right?"

"Yeah."

"Okay, go get changed. I'll meet you at the car."

"Okay."

My dad was always in the stands during practices and games. Other than the time he was in Europe, he never missed a single one. It felt good to have him there. But what I appreciated even more was that he didn't overstep. He never talked to my coaches about my role on the team or anything like that. Everything I had earned as a basketball player up to that point was because of my hard work and skill. My dad didn't want anything handed to me and I didn't either.

It was already dark out when I stepped out of school and waited on the front steps for my dad to pull the car around. Most of my other teammates were on their way home already, either taking the bus or walking home. I was the only one on the team who didn't live in the city.

I heard the door open behind me and it was Sherrod.

"What you doin'?" he said.

"Just waiting for my dad."

Dorrell and another teammate walked outside just then.

"Sherrod," Dorrell said. "This motherfucker ain't even from Detroit. He from the suburbs."

"Shut up, Dorrell," Sherrod said.

Dorrell stood in front of me.

"He ain't even black," he laughed. "I bet if you slice open that little Oreo, he got a white creamy filling inside."

I took both my fists and jammed them into his skinny chest. I could hear him gasp a little when his back slammed into the metal door. Sherrod grabbed my shoulders with both arms and pulled me off Dorrell.

Sherrod got in between us as Dorrell stood straight and fixed the collar of his hoodie that was bunched up around his neck.

"You niggas need to chill," Sherrod said.

"This little motherfucker needs to know his place!" Dorrell said.

"Shut up," Sherrod said.

My dad pulled up in the Mercedes. We all looked over at it.

"Watch your back," Dorrell said, as he and the other teammate started down the steps.

"Punk," I said, breathing hard and staring even harder at him.

He walked down the stairs backwards, smiling at me the whole way. He finally turned around, passed my dad's car, and left campus.

"Don't worry about him," Sherrod said, with a pat on my back. "He's just worried that you're about to take his job."

I didn't say anything. I needed to cool down first.

Sherrod waved to my dad and in response, he beeped the horn.

"Yo, I bet it was cool going to Pistons games when he played for them? I bet that was real cool."

"It was . . ."

I looked over his shoulder at the Mercedes. I looked back to him and he was looking straight in my eyes, waiting for my response.

"It was cool," I said. "It made me feel like anything was possible."

"Yeah," he said. "That's my dream right there, to play for the Pistons. The Palace of Auburn Hills. Damn." He smiled. "Shit, don't get me wrong," he said. "I'll play for any team in the NBA. Any team that drafts me. But one day, I want to play for the Pistons. No doubt about that."

"I think you'll make it."

"Long ways from that," he said.

My dad beeped the horn again, this time, for me to come to the car.

"I'm gettin' ready to catch this bus," Sherrod said, as he switched his gym bag over to his other shoulder.

"Where do you live?"

"Off Livernois and Chicago."

I didn't say anything because I knew what that meant.

"No place good," he said, shaking his head. "No place good."

We dapped.

"See you tomorrow," he said, before starting down the steps.

"Sherrod!"

He turned around.

"You need a ride?" I said. "It's cold and my dad'll be happy—"

"Nah, I'm good," he said. "Thanks."

I nodded and before he walked off school property, he flashed a peace sign towards the Mercedes. My dad smiled back to him from behind the driver's side window.

I got into the car.

"I told Sherrod that we'd give him a ride but he said no."

"Why didn't you insist?" he said. "Let's go see if we can catch him."

"I tried. He said that he would catch the bus."

He pulled the car off school grounds and made a right onto Vernor. Sherrod was nowhere to be found.

"Missed him," I said.

"Next time, don't ask Sherrod," he said. "Just tell him. If you want to do something good for someone, don't ask them. You just gotta do it."

"Okay."

We got onto the highway towards Auburn Hills.

"Dorrell was talking shit again, I see."

"It's nothing," I said. "The most annoying part is that he thinks I'm not black enough because I live in Auburn Hills."

My dad stayed silent as he switched to the fast lane.

"Livernois and Chicago," I said. "That's the worst part of Detroit, right?"

"So?"

"Can you take me over there one night after practice? I want to see what it's like. Sherrod and Dorrell live there. Most of the team does."

He shook his head. "Boy, I worked my entire life to not have to go into neighborhoods like that ever again."

"I just want to see why these guys don't think I'm hard enough."

"Guys? I thought it was just Dorrell talking shit?"

"Now it's just Dorrell. But he's not the first to say it. And he won't be the last either."

"Look, Isaiah, you don't need to live in places like that to be 'hard,'" he said. "You kids listen to that shit that passes for music these days and think it's glamorous. The hard life. The street life."

He looked me right in the eyes.

"Let me tell you something. It's not glamorous. And it doesn't end good. Stories like mine and Sherrod's. They're not common. The streets will always have a good record when it comes to swallowing up young niggas."

"It's not even worth seeing?" I said. "Just to experience it?"

"Experience what?" he said. "You wanna see drug addicts? You might get lucky and see someone get shot or cut up. Does that make you tough? Will that make you hard? You don't need to see that shit, Isaiah. I've worked hard so that you don't have to see that shit."

SIX

Practice was cancelled the next day because of a tragedy. This was my first taste of the streets, and honestly, it made me sick.

Sherrod was shot and killed the night before in front of his apartment building, about an hour after our first practice of the season and a few hours after we talked on the front steps of school. The police had already caught the guy who killed him; the man was looking for Sherrod's older brother, Kennard, who had been in and out of jail for dealing.

All of Sherrod's hard work meant nothing now. His dream of playing for the Pistons was gone.

Who knows? I may have been the last person to have a conversation with him before his life ended.

Coach called an emergency meeting in the gym at the beginning of school. He gave us the few details there were about Sherrod's murder—the saddest one being that Sherrod paid the price for simply looking like his brother. Once Coach began to talk, his eyes watered and his voice choked. He put his hands up suddenly and said that he didn't have anything else to say except that Sherrod was one of his favorite players that he had ever coached. He looked broken.

That was the moment where a guilty feeling washed over me. I should've insisted on taking Sherrod home instead of just asking. Maybe, things would've turned out differently. I'm not sure how, but I couldn't escape the feeling that I failed somehow.

The rest of the guys left the gym and I stayed behind, sitting in a dark corner. We didn't know if we were even going to play the season out. I didn't care about that right then. I needed to hear that I didn't have any fault in Sherrod's death.

The school day went by without any feeling. Every class blended in with the others. Everyone inside those walls was sad: players, students, and teachers. I went to the bathroom during lunch to shed a few tears myself. I was looking forward to playing alongside Sherrod. I wanted to help him take our team to an unexpected championship. Most of all, I wanted to be his friend.

I needed to talk to Coach after school. We didn't have practice, but I knew he'd be in his office. I knocked on his door and there he was, sitting behind his desk with his face in his hands.

He looked up and his face was red, eyes puffed. He waved a hand weakly at a seat in front of his desk.

"Isaiah," he said, in a low voice.

"Coach," I said. "I need to talk to you."

"What is it?"

"I feel like Sherrod's death was my fault."

"What?"

His eyes were questioning me, but still very sad.

"What do you mean?" he asked.

"After practice, I was talking with him outside the locker room and I offered a ride home from my dad."

He didn't say anything.

"I can't help but think that if we had given him a ride, his life wouldn't be over," I said.

"Isaiah," he said. "It's not your fault. Not at all." A tear streamed down the side of his face.

"It's the world's fault. Plain and simple."

He smashed a fist on his desk and its legs rattled against the hard floor.

"Thanks, Coach," I said.

He nodded and his silence told me that it was time to leave the office. I waved to him and walked out feeling a little better. But I still needed to hear that I wasn't at fault from someone else. I needed to hear it from my dad.

The sky was gray as I waited for my dad outside

of school. My mind was blank as I stared up at the heavy sky. Sherrod's death clouded everything.

My dad pulled up, parked, and got out of the car. As he walked over to me, his sad eyes met mine. He gave me a hug, almost squeezing the life out of me. Neither of us said anything.

My dad passed the exit to Auburn Hills.

"I'm not working out right now," I said.

"We're not going to the gym."

Downtown Detroit passed by us. The skyscrapers did their best with the grey skies that were given to them.

We were in a neighborhood that I didn't know. But when I saw the street signs, I knew where we were headed. My dad swung a left onto Livernois and we continued driving for a few blocks. The streets looked damaged, like the ones you see on the news in places where wars have been fought. There were more vacants than anywhere else I'd seen in the city. The streets were empty for the most part, with the only action happening out in front of the occasional liquor store. My dad took a right onto Chicago Street and it was more of the same, maybe even worse. There was trash everywhere and the grass grew in wild brown-green patches. It started to drizzle, really emptying the streets now, except for a group of young kids playing on a patch of concrete between two vacants.

We pulled up to another apartment building that was falling apart, but at least it looked like people still lived there. He put the car in park and looked over at me. There was yellow tape, stuck to the front door of the building, flapping in the wind.

I looked back at him.

"Tell me it's not my fault."

"What's not your fault, son?"

I nodded to the building.

"Sherrod's murder?" he said. "Are you crazy?"

"The ride."

"No, Isaiah," he said, with a tremble in his voice. He touched the back of my head and for a moment, I thought that he was going to cry.

"No. No. No."

He took a deep breath in and let the air out through his mouth.

"It's hard to say whose fault it is, son," he said. "But it sure ain't not yours."

I looked over to the building again. The wind had died and the yellow police tape rested.

My dad put the car in drive and we drove home to Auburn Hills in silence.

SEVEN

"You want some breakfast, Honey?" my mom said, standing in my doorway the next morning.

She wore a smile on her face, and that made me feel a little bit better about things. Seeing her up on her feet did too.

"Yeah," I said.

First thing she did when we got downstairs was crack four eggs in a bowl. Next, she put a few strips of bacon into a frying pan.

I poured the orange juice.

"I have some bad news," I said.

She put the wooden spoon down on the stove and looked at me with a knowing smile.

"What?" I said.

"Go on," she said.

"This kid on my team," I said. "The best player on the team, actually. He was shot the night before last. He's dead."

"I heard," she said. Tears welled up in my eyes and suddenly they were filled. She came close, grabbed hold of me and hugged me tight. I put my arms around her and squeezed back. It felt good to be hugged by her. By the time we let go, her eyes were wet too.

She wiped her eyes and turned the heat down on the frying pan. The smell of bacon filled the kitchen and that simple thing made me feel good. It gave me hope that I would have my mother back.

"Your father told me about it last night."

"Dad didn't come in after he dropped me off."

"He called."

She stirred some milk into the eggs and then dropped them into another pan. They sizzled before she turned the heat underneath them to low.

"He said that you were feeling like you had something to do with it," she said. "Well, just like Dad told you, you had nothing to do with it. It's that city—it's just," she paused, "I don't know."

"I know, Mom," I said.

"And it's natural to feel that way," she said. "It's natural to connect it to yourself. But the truth is, you're not a part of that story. He could've talked to anybody else on the team right before he got on that bus. It just happened to be you."

"We were becoming friends, too," I said. "I've never known anybody around my age who has died."

"You're lucky," she said.

She flipped the bacon and scrambled the eggs. I watched her as she did these things and it looked like something inside of her had changed. She fixed two plates and set one in front of me and then one in front of herself. She poured herself a coffee and sat across from me as we ate.

"Things have been off for a while around here,

Isaiah," she said. "And I want you to know that I'm going to fix my part in it. Things are gonna go back to the way they used to be."

Early in my life, before basketball became a huge part of it, my dad was away a lot and I was with my mom at all times. And she was great. She was my best friend. She always made sure that I was safe and fed. My dad always said that the close relationship between my mom and me made him happy. His mom left his dad when he was just two years old. That's also why at the beginning of their marriage, he didn't want my mother to work. So she didn't.

When he left for Europe to extend his playing career, he didn't take us. He thought that dragging us all around Europe would be worse than us being apart. I didn't remember much about the time that he was in Europe, other than missing him and feeling really close to my mom.

As I got older and basketball took up the majority of my time, my dad started taking a bigger role in my life. Every year, my mom seemed to get a little sadder, and her presence in my life faded a little more. I guessed that my dad got fed up with it. I only ever heard his side of the story. He complained that she didn't have a path—that there was nothing in her life that she wanted to work for. He often boasted that when he made it out of the projects of Boston, he saved two lives: his and hers.

I decided that I had to hear her side.

I hit her with the question.

"Is Dad coming back to live here?"

She shook her head.

"Isaiah—"

"Something's happening, Mom," I said. "I know it."

"Happening with what, Isaiah?"

"Us," I said. "What's happened to us? To our family?"

She didn't say anything. She just stared at me without blinking her eyes.

"Dad doesn't live here anymore. I know that. I guess I just want to know why."

She still couldn't say it. I could see some kind of pain in her eyes and face.

I looked around the empty kitchen that fed into the empty den that led to the big, empty living room.

"You're asleep all the time," I said. "You didn't even come to *one* of my games last season. You used to at least come to all the home games."

"I'm tired, Isaiah," she said. "Tired of basketball. Tired of your father."

"Are you tired of me?"

The tears came back into her eyes. "No, Honey," she said, "I could never get tired of you."

"It seems like the opposite," I said.

She wiped the tears out of her eyes and sighed. She continued looking right at me and it didn't make me feel uncomfortable. It actually felt good. It felt good that she was up and out of bed and sitting with me.

"Why is Dad gone?" I said, almost shouting it. "I want us to be a family again. I want Dad here and I want my mom back."

"You're all grown up, Isaiah," she said. "You're not a kid anymore."

"So tell me."

"You have to ask him," she said. "You're old enough to understand. But it has to come from him. He has to tell you."

Sure, my dad was around. It seemed like I was still missing him, though. Like he was there— but not there—at the same time. I especially needed him now after what happened to Sherrod. And not just to talk about basketball or to work on my game. I wanted to ask him about girls. I wanted him to teach me how to shave. Sometimes, I even wanted a hug from him before I went to bed.

"I tried, Isaiah," she said, snapping me back into the moment. "It's not for a lack of trying."

She leaned over and gave me another hug. I rested my head on her shoulder.

They weren't fighting hard enough to stay together and keep our roots strong. I had to find out what the hell was going on, and fast.

EIGHT

We had the weekend off as Coach thought about Sherrod and the prospect of going forward without him. I didn't see my dad that entire weekend and spent all the time with my mom instead. It felt like the old days. It felt good. She cooked for me and we even went to a movie on Sunday night—an old family tradition. There was only one person missing to make things complete. I had to try to make us whole again, even if they weren't going to.

On Monday morning, we switched things up and my mom drove me to school. My dad and I planned to work out that evening. And that's when I would ask him.

The first school day after Sherrod's death was a bitter one, both indoors and out. On the outside, the temperature was below freezing, the sky a dull gray, and inside of school the mood was still one of shock and devastation.

There was a weight on my shoulders that day, going from classroom to classroom. My legs were heavy, like they were in quicksand. I was sweating too, for some reason, and yet my mouth was dry, even after drinking three bottles of water. Instead of lunch, I went to see the nurse. She checked my temperature and said I was fine. I told her that I didn't feel fine and she replied that it was probably all in my head.

As an alternative to going back to class like I was supposed to, I cruised the halls. There was nowhere else to go. I walked by the gym and it was dark. I went inside and stood at mid-court, looking up to the rafters at the retired jerseys of some of

Detroit's finest. All of them came from the kind of neighborhood that Sherrod came from. None of them came from the suburbs.

The door to the gym swung open and I turned around, assuming it was going to be someone to tell me to get back to class. But there was no authority figure there. It was two of my teammates, Derrick and Tishaun. They were both juniors from the city, on scholarship. Derrick was a bench player—who never got in the games—from the championship team the season before, and Tishaun was a starter on the JV team during that same season. From my view, both of them were bench players on this year's team.

"What you doing in here?" Tishaun said.

"I don't know," I said. "I had to get out of class."

"Season's probably off," he said. "Coach didn't even come in today."

"So we figure," Derrick said, "if Coach ain't here, we shouldn't be here either."

"What do you mean?" I said.

"We're gonna bounce out of here," Tishaun said.

"Where are you guys gonna go?" I said.

"My boy is throwing a little party back around the way," Derrick said.

"A party on Monday morning?" I said.

They laughed.

"You ain't used to the projects, is you?" Derrick said. "It don't have to be the weekend to break out."

"You in?" Tishaun said.

"Now?" I said.

"Yeah," Derrick said. "We're gonna catch the eight mile and hop off on Mack."

"I'm not sure," I said. "If we get caught—"

"They not gonna say shit to us," Derrick said. "They can't touch us after what happened to Sherrod."

Somehow that made sense. But it wasn't what sealed the deal for me. I thought about Dorrell's taunts, that I wasn't black enough because I lived out in suburbs. If my dad wouldn't show me the streets of Detroit, I would have to go explore them myself.

"All right," I said. "I'll go."

"Aight, come on," Derrick said.

We snuck out of the locker room exit. It spit us out of a door into the back parking lot. We weaved through the luxury cars belonging to the students that actually paid to go to school there. Even though I was from the suburbs and rode to school in a luxury car, I never felt a part of the private school world. And that was because of basketball. The guys on the hoops team were scholarship kids—from the real streets of Detroit. The rest of the school—they were just visiting.

Basketball allowed me to be something I was not. If not for basketball, there'd be no seeing Detroit for me. So Dorrell was right in that sense. I probably would have been in some private school in Auburn Hills, unaware of the city thirty miles south. Until that day, my interactions with the city of Detroit had been safe and controlled. Mostly behind the walls of some prep school.

The seventeen bus, or "Eight Mile" as it was called, pulled up to its stop and we hopped on using the back door. The bus smelled like pee and I covered my nose with the collar of my sweatshirt. All of the passengers on the bus were black except the Hispanic driver. I looked out of the window and didn't recognize where I was. The streets were cold and empty, aside from a few guys standing outside of a corner store or two. There were broken down cars on blocks, and this was in Detroit— the place where cars used be built. Like Sherrod's neighborhood, and the one near the gym, there were vacants on every block. I counted as many as I could before it became ridiculous.

"What's up with those vacants?" I said.

"Whatchu mean?" Derrick said.

"People live in there?" I said.

"Hell, yeah, they do," Derrick replied.

"Nah, them vacants is nasty," Tishaun said. "Addicts be shootin' up and takin' shits in them."

"Shut yo' dumb ass up!" Derrick said. "What you know about the vacants?"

"Nigga, how you know what goes on in them?" Tishaun fired back.

"'Cause I used to live in one," he said, without any shame on his face. "Now shut your little young ass up!"

That shut Tishaun up.

"Why you wanna know, Isaiah?" Derrick said, turning away from Tishaun.

"Just curious," I said. "I see them all over town. It doesn't make sense that they don't fix them up. I mean, people need places to live and there are all these empty houses."

Derrick didn't say anything to that. Tishaun was too scared to. The rest of the bus ride was silent until we got off at Mack and Preston.

We walked a few blocks and then went into a corner store. Derrick bought a couple of blunts and asked me to chip in for the forties. I put a couple of dollars in even though I didn't want to drink beer. I also bought myself a Gatorade.

After a few more minutes down Mack, we turned right onto a small street that had a set of row houses. I counted nine vacants out of the set of ten on the block. The one that wasn't vacant was clearly the "party" house. Bass thumped from inside. Derrick led us up the front steps and the actual music behind the bass came through. He pounded on the door a few times.

A big man with big arms underneath a white thermal answered. He smiled when he saw Derrick.

"What up, homie?" he said.

They dapped up and Derrick pointed back to us.

"These are a couple of the young 'uns from the squad," he said. "Tishaun and Isaiah."

Derek then pointed to the big man.

"This is Sean," he said. "It's his spot."

We clapped hands with Sean and he stepped

aside to let us in. Derrick led the way downstairs, into the basement where the music was coming from.

It was a big basement. There were around ten people down there. Five were girls—they talked amongst themselves at a table, beers resting in front of them, while the guys laughed and played dominoes at another table and drank from red plastic cups.

The basement was nice, to my surprise. The heat worked and it was cranked up to battle the freezing temperature. I didn't expect that the one active house in a row of vacants would have a basement that was finished, let alone working heat. There were a couple of big, comfortable-looking couches against a wall across from where all the people were. A big screen TV stood in the corner, opposite the couches. The basement reminded me of my basement back in Auburn Hills. That surprised me too—that I could feel the same in one of the poorest neighborhoods in Detroit as I did in my home in the suburbs.

None of the partygoers reacted to us. They continued having their own fun. For a little while, we just stood around and I tried not to stare too much.

There was a table set up in one of the other corners of the basement. It had bottles of liquor set on top. Derrick walked over in its direction and Tishaun and I followed. Derrick put the forties that we bought inside a cooler underneath the table.

"Whatchu want?" he asked.

"Lemme get a beer," Tishaun said. "They got Miller High Life?"

"Yeah," he said.

He handed Tishaun a bottle and he twisted the cap off. He took a sip and went to take a seat on of the couches.

"What about you?"

"I never drank before," I said.

"Your dad never gave you a sip of his beer?"

Derrick's question made me realize that I had never even seen my dad take a sip of alcohol. Come to think of it, no one in my house drank. Knowing my dad, he probably had a rule that my mother couldn't drink while she was in the house. It made sense. My dad was sensitive to the fact that he worked hard to make it out of the projects. He viewed drugs and alcohol as things that got in the way of escaping the ghetto. So he never drank. And he definitely wouldn't want me drinking.

"No," I said.

"Shit," he said, with a chuckle. "That's the only thing my dad ever taught me."

"How can you ball so good if you drink?" I said. "I mean, do you drink all the time?"

"I usually don't drink during the season," he said. "But with Sherrod getting killed and shit, we might not even have a season."

"I'm good," I said, clutching my Gatorade. "I'll just drink this."

"Aight," he said, as he grabbed a Miller High Life and cracked it open.

I sat down next to Tishaun. Derrick went over to the domino game. The couch was as comfortable as it looked.

"You sure you don't wanna beer?" Tishaun said.

"No," I said.

Sean walked downstairs with a thick blunt behind his ear.

"Who wants to hit this shit?" he said, to the whole room.

The ladies screamed and laughed and the guys just smirked, barely looking up from their game.

Sean approached us.

"What about you young 'uns?"

"Yeah," Tishaun said. "Blaze it."

Derrick joined us over at the couch. He tapped me on the shoulder.

"This shit is the bomb," he said.

Sean lit the blunt and the smell of it hit me right in the face. It smelled like a skunk. Sean took a couple of puffs and passed it to Tishaun. Tishaun took two little hits and started coughing. He held it out to me and I didn't reach for it.

"You ain't gonna hit it?" Derrick said.

"Nah, man," I said.

I could feel my dad there, even though I knew he wasn't anywhere near the party. There was this feeling I had inside of me, that if I took a puff, or a sip, I'd be letting him down. Letting my father down wasn't the whole story. I also felt that if did those things, it'd make things even worse at home. I thought about my dad blaming my mom if he found out that I drank and smoked. Even if it was just one time, he'd blame her. Then he'd label me a lazy bum.

"Pass that shit over here, nigga," Derrick said.

He greedily took the blunt from Tishaun, took a few hits, and passed it back to Sean. Derrick looked like a pro at this, not coughing once and letting the smoke flow out of his throat peacefully. Tishaun was still coughing after his two, little hits.

There was a haze of smoke in the basement and it affected me even though I didn't take one hit. I looked around the room and it started to spin. Everything felt fuzzy. This was not good for me, because I was so used to feeling sharp and alert.

Everyone else was comfortable, except me. And it made sense. I was out of my comfort zone, while everyone else looked like they were taking part in a daily routine.

I needed to get out of that basement. The air was hot and musty and I was sweating underneath my winter clothes. I bolted up from the couch and could feel Derrick and Tishaun staring at me.

"Whatchu doing?" Derrick said. He smacked Tishaun's shoulder. "This nigga is high and didn't take a single hit."

They laughed.

"I need to get some air," I said.

"You ain't gonna get that here in Detroit," Derrick said. "Better go to back Auburn Hills, or better yet, Canada."

They laughed again, this time with bitterness.

"I'll be right back," I said.

I took the stairs two at a time and blasted out of the front door. I took three deep breaths out on the doorstep and the cold air actually helped me start to feel normal.

I looked back at the house and the bass continued to thump. I jammed my hands in my pockets and started down the block. I studied the vacants as I passed by them. The windows on most of them were busted out, and the ones that weren't had boards in their place. All of the front doorways had boards in place of doors. Not all of the old homes were crumbling to the ground, though. I counted five out of the nine vacants on the block that looked sturdy and livable.

The worst looking one was at the far end of the block. I stood in front of it for a few minutes, just staring at it. I wanted to know if there was someone inside. And if so, I wanted to know why they were in there. Usually, I'd be driving through the city with my dad on my way back home to Auburn Hills when these questions came to mind. But now, I was standing right in front of a vacant, without my dad in sight.

I walked up the stairs to the front door. There was the smell of garbage, but I wasn't sure if the smell was coming from the house or from the garbage on the street. I put a hand on the board covering the front door and it was cold and smooth. I grasped at the board with two hands and found a good grip. I threw my body weight back and pulled as hard as I could. The board creaked and then gave out. I ripped it off the doorway and when I looked inside, nothing moved or said anything. There was just blackness staring back at me. I took a step inside. I'm not sure why I did that. I don't even know what I was doing there, in one of the worst parts of Detroit. Something deep down inside was telling me that I was on a mission.

Everything was dusty through the doorway, and the smell was horrendous—a mixture of urine and mold. I covered my nose again with my sweatshirt. There was a table in the center of that front room, which, from the looks of the hollowed-out stove in the corner, used to be the kitchen. There were three burnt-out candles on top of the table, along with two bent spoons and a syringe. Tishaun was right. Drug addicts were making use of the vacants.

Was that the case with all of them?

"Hey! What are you doing in there?" a heavy, clear voice said from behind. "Put your hands up!"

I slowly put my hands up and slowly turned around.

It was a cop. A black cop. He was tall, bald, and his muscles showed through his uniform, even through all the layers. He stood at the doorway, looking in. He had a hand on his gun but didn't pull it. His eyes were sharp.

"What are you doing?" he said, a little less fierce than before.

"I, uh. I—"

"Where do you live?"

"I live in," I said, shook. "I live in Auburn Hills."

He chuckled. "Bullshit you do."

"No I do. It's the truth."

"Okay, get on out of there."

I walked out of the vacant and followed him to his car. The radio inside beeped and cracked through the closed window. He opened the driver's side door, grabbed the radio and spoke some kind of code into it. While he waited for a response, he looked to me.

"Okay," he said. "What's going on here? This isn't making a whole lot of sense."

"I go to school in the city. I play basketball and a couple of my teammates and me cut school and came down here for a party. I left the party to go back to school."

His eyes said didn't believe any of it. "And on the way back to the bus you decided to peel back the wood on a vacant and take a look inside?"

I didn't respond.

"You trying to get killed?" he asked me.

"No sir," I responded.

"Then don't go poking your head in a vacant house." He paused, and then sighed. "All right, lemme take you back to school. No need to call your parents in on this. Get in," he said, with a nod to the passenger's side.

I got into the car, feeling lucky.

The radio sounded off with a robbery attempt in another neighborhood.

"You said you play basketball?"

"Yes."

"I played too," he said. "At Mercy. A long, long time ago."

"What position?"

"Off guard," he said. "But you probably know it as shooting guard."

"I've heard it said that way."

"Lemme ask you something," he said. "Why'd you go inside the vacant?"

The radio went off again with another crime in another neighborhood.

"I don't know," I said. "I just wanted to see what was inside."

He stared at me for a moment and then put his eyes back on the road.

"It's weird that there are so many empty houses in the city," I said.

He nodded and kept his eyes on the road.

"Can I ask you a question?"

"Sure," he said.

"Are the vacants only used by drug addicts?"

"Mostly," he said. "But not all. Homeless people use them too."

"How can there be homeless people in the city if there are so many empty houses?" I said. "Can't the houses be fixed up and used for the homeless?

"That's a good question," he said. "Maybe you should run for Mayor."

"It's messed up."

"It is," he said. "It sure is."

There weren't many more words exchanged on the ride back to school. The radio came alive a couple more times; the last call alerted all officers to a murder that happened in the same South Detroit neighborhood where Sherrod was killed a few nights before.

He shook his head. "South Detroit is burning."

I asked him to drop me off a couple of blocks away from school. I didn't want to create a scene by showing up to school in a police car. He was cool and told me that would be okay.

He pulled over to the curb and put the car in park a few blocks north of school.

"Hold on," he said. "Your school is right up there off Vernor, right?"

I nodded.

"Your teammate is the one who was killed last week then?"

I nodded again.

"What a pointless fuckin' tragedy," he said. "He was a good player. And from the sound of it, a good kid too."

I didn't say anything to that.

"Well, what did you learn out in the South Side today?"

"What did I learn?"

"Yeah what did you learn?"

"I learned that it's not so bad living in Auburn Hills."

"Good," he said.

I got out of the car and walked back to school. The clouds cleared up and sun was bright now. The air warmed up a little too. I snuck back into school as easily as I snuck out. I got back just in time for the last class of the day: art. When I sat down at my desk, a white classmate, who was dropped off to school in a BMW every morning, asked me where I had been all day. I told him I was out getting schooled. When he asked what I meant by that, I told him to hop on the Eight Mile heading south, get off at Mack and he could learn something too.

NINE

After school, Coach gathered the team in the locker room for a surprise meeting. Tishaun was wrong. Coach *was* in his office all day. His eyes and nose were red, and when he spoke, his voice was low and still shaken. Derrick and Tishaun didn't make it back to school for the meeting. When Coach asked if anybody had seen them, we all responded with a collective "no."

Derrick *was* right, Coach wasn't upset with their absences.

"I thought a lot over the weekend," Coach said. "And there are still a lot of things to think about. But with regards to the season . . ."

He paused and looked around the locker room.

"The best way to honor Sherrod would be to play. And win for him."

He then asked us if we were up to it.

We all said that we were.

"Okay," he said, with something resembling a smile. "Practice will start up again after school tomorrow. I want you all to take one more night to reflect on Sherrod's death. Then when we start back up tomorrow, we'll begin celebrating his life. Together."

I looked around the room at the other guys, and everyone seemed like they were moved by Coach's words. Even Dorrell dropped the hard attitude and softened his eyes.

"One more thing. When you get home, I want all of you to write down your goals for the season and bring them in tomorrow. You're gonna read them out loud before practice. For some of you, the goals that you write down tonight might be very different from the ones you had at the beginning of the season, before this happened."

Coach looked around again and locked eyes with me.

"But that's life," he said. "You have to adapt. Adjust."

He dismissed us after that. But before I could leave, he pulled me aside to talk one-on-one. He waited for the rest of the team to exit the locker room. Dorrell eyed me as he walked out.

"You're gonna be my starting point guard, Isaiah."

I was ready for this. There was no easing into a starting role now. Sherrod's death had sped everything up.

"I'm also naming you team captain. Along with Derrick," he said. "I'm gonna let the team know tomorrow. I just wanted to make sure you're up for it."

I thought about Derrick getting high and drunk at the house party, but didn't say anything.

"I am up for it, Coach."

"Derrick will lead with experience and you'll lead with your work ethic."

I nodded and smiled for the first time in what felt like weeks.

"We're only gonna go as far as you take us," he said. "Without Sherrod, it's the only way."

"Thank you, Coach."

"Go home and write those goals down," he said. "Yours will be the most different."

He patted me on the shoulder and walked towards his office. I took a seat in front of Sherrod's locker. On one hand, I was excited to be given all that responsibility. But there was also a feeling of guilt. Sherrod's death had given me this opportunity to be a team leader.

I came up with my new goals for the season right there, in front of Sherrod's locker. The first was to play the season for Sherrod. That was a no-brainer. The second one was a little more selfish. I planned on putting the team on my back. Forget about simply being named the starting point guard. That was nothing to me. My team needed something more. They needed someone to give them hope that the season still had a chance to be special. Without Sherrod, I was the only one who could give them that hope.

There were footsteps from behind and I turned to see my dad standing in the doorway of the locker room.

He nodded and his eyes were inquisitive. "Season on?"

———

"That's great news," my dad said, as we pulled onto the ramp towards Auburn Hills. "Being named starting point guard—*and* captain—on the same day. That never happened to me. I'm proud of you, son."

"Thanks, Dad."

"Let's hit the gym."

"Sure."

The sky was dull, the color of pencil lead. It was time to talk to my dad about what was going on at home. My good news softened the mood a little and there was no better time to have the talk.

"Mom is not doing so good," I said.

He looked over at me with raised eyebrows.

"What do you mean?"

"I mean she's not doing good. She's not . . . she's not my mom anymore."

"I thought you guys had a good weekend."

"It was good," I said. "But you were missing. I want you back at home. I want us all to be under the same roof again."

He just shook his head. The only sound in the car came from the engine, roaring as we picked up speed.

"Are you and Mom getting a divorce?"

He didn't answer right away. He kept both hands on the steering wheel and sighed deeply.

"Yes, son," he said. "We can't save it."

The words crushed me. I turned my head away from him and looked out my window. I felt like crying. I wanted to cry but somehow held it in. I bit my lip, trying not to look weak in front my dad. We didn't talk on the rest of the ride. I just stared out of the window, feeling like the sky was coming down on me.

TEN

"Thanks for not sayin' anything to Coach," Derrick said, as he caught up with me in the hall the next morning before school.

I just nodded as we walked. The two captains of the basketball team, side by side.

"The party got crazy after you bounced," he said. "Why'd you just leave like that?"

"I don't know," I said. "It wasn't feeling right."

"It's all good, Isaiah," he said, stopping in front of his first period classroom. "You showed me that I can trust you. And now that we're both captains, we'll lead the team all the way. Together."

He held out his fist for a bump. I barely raised mine.

"Whatever, Derrick," I said, before walking off and leaving him in front of the classroom.

From the party, I could see what kind of leader Derrick was going to be. I didn't need or want his help with anything.

———

School went by fast that day. I didn't remember a single thing from any of my classes. I couldn't focus because of what my dad told me the day before.

Practice couldn't come soon enough. I couldn't wait to let it all out.

During last period though, I remembered that I had forgotten to write my goals for the season. After I had found out my parents were getting divorced, I just went to my room, shut the door and got in bed. I ignored my responsibilities—homework, writing my goals down. I even blew off the work-out with my dad.

I looked up at the clock and there wasn't much time left before practice. I had to hurry.

After last bell, I found a quiet hallway to sit down and write.

———

Coach brought us up in a circle at half court before practice. Everyone was there—including Derrick and Tishaun. Everyone, except Sherrod.

"Okay, guys," he said, "Time to share our goals. Actually, I should probably do this first. Isaiah. Derrick. Come over here."

Derrick and I broke away from the rest of the guys and walked over next to Coach.

"Isaiah and Derrick are going to be our captains this year," he said. "We usually have three of them. But we're going to leave one of the spots for Sherrod."

He choked up and looked down to the floor for a moment.

"It's going to be tough without him, both on and off the floor. But if we come together, we can win. And we have to win for Sherrod."

He paused again to make sure that there would be no tears.

"Isaiah, can you share your goals for the season with us?"

I unfolded the sheet of paper that I had just written on. I cleared my throat.

"I have three goals for this season," I said. "The first one is to be the best teammate I can be. That means I'm gonna share the basketball and run back as fast as I can on defense. Goal number two is to not miss a practice. It's important to be out there day in and day out and I don't just mean for games. And goal number three is to get out in the community of Detroit and do some good. I think that will be the best way to pay tribute to Sherrod."

Dorrell rolled his eyes and was the only one

of my teammates who didn't clap after I finished talking.

I walked back over to the rest of my teammates, but stood away from Dorrell. He was the only one who didn't believe in me. I would have to make him a believer.

"Thank you, Isaiah," coach said. "Derrick, you're up. Give us your goals."

———

The beginning of practice was intense. There was a lot energy and emotion that we needed to get out. We went at each other hard. I targeted Dorrell. Any time he was up in a drill, I cut in line to go against him. Anytime I defended him, I made sure to be a little extra physical.

Guys were diving on the floor for loose balls. Guys were flying all over the place on defense. If we played like that during the season, we wouldn't lose many games. It was fun to be out there competing.

During a three-on-two drill, where I was on offense and Dorrell was on defense, I dribbled the ball straight down the middle of the lane, faked a pass to the left—which Dorrell bit on—and passed the ball to a streaking teammate on the right, who made a layup off the glass. I smiled at Dorrell and shook my head.

"You better watch your ankles," I said, before turning my back on him and starting down to the other end of the floor.

"Shut the fuck up," he said, from behind.

Next thing I knew, there were two hands on my back. He pushed me as hard as he could and because I was already moving forward, I almost fell on my face. I turned around and tried to go after him. But the rest of guys got between us.

Coach blew his whistle and stopped practice.

"Dorrell! Isaiah!" he said. "What the hell is the matter with you two?"

I didn't say anything. I just stared at Dorrell.

"This weak ass punk from the suburbs has been

talkin' shit all practice and throwin' little elbows and shit," he said. "Why don't you come see me after practice and I'll show you how we do it in the D!"

Coach went straight over to Dorrell and got in his face.

"Keep quiet, Dorrell!" he said.

He took a deep breath as things cooled down in the steamy gym. He looked around at all the guys and his eyes stopped when they got to me.

"I'm not gonna put up with this. Not now. Not ever," he said.

I could feel myself relax and my breathing became normal. Dorrell chilled out too. But his eyes were still angry.

"We're all we got!" Coach said. "Look around this gym. Take a good god damn look!" he said, and his voice echoed in the empty gym. "This little group right here—this is it. If you want to be winners you have to trust each other. You have to love each other."

He looked around at us one last time.

"Isaiah. Dorrell. You guys need to shake. Put this nonsense to bed."

I stepped up first, while Dorrell hesitated. I looked him right in the eyes as we shook hands. He did the same. But it wasn't over yet. Not by a long shot.

My first practice as a starter and team captain was not going the way I expected it to. Going after Dorrell like I had was a selfish—and probably a stupid—thing to do. But I just wanted to get him off my back. Without Sherrod here to play peacemaker, I wasn't sure if Dorrell and I would ever get along.

It was yet to be seen whether the death of our best player and leader would bring us closer together. If that first practice was any indication, it was probably gonna tear us apart.

ELEVEN

The car ride home from practice was tense. My dad was on edge because I was on edge. It didn't help that I had just come to blows with one of my teammates.

"You just gotta punch him in the mouth once," he said. "That's the only way he'll quit."

"I'll take care of it," I said, sharply.

"Oh, *you* will?"

I didn't know if I could take care of the situation with Dorrell, or if there was even a way to take care of it. But what I didn't want was to hear from my dad. He was a person who made his way out of the projects in Boston to the NBA, and he didn't even have the strength—or the heart—to keep the family together.

"You don't need to worry about it," I said. "Worry about yourself."

"Boy, you better watch who you're talking to like that," he said. "I'm not one of your little punk-ass teammates."

We were both quiet on the rest of the ride. He dropped me off and pulled out of the driveway before I even walked in the house. I knew my dad. He was a prideful man. My words had stung him because they were true. Deep down inside, I hoped that my words would change him. That he would turn his car back around, park it in the driveway, and walk into the house. *His* house.

———

"Isaiah," my mom said. "You're not eating at all. Aren't you hungry?"

"Not so much," I said, without looking up at her.

Things were better around the house. My mom was out of her room and up on her feet, doing things for me like I was used to. But the house still had an empty feel. It would never be the same, unless my dad came home.

"What's wrong?"

"I talked to Dad yesterday, on the way home from school."

"It must've not been good," she said. "You went straight to your room and didn't come out until the morning."

"He said that you guys are getting divorced. And that there's no way to fix it."

She didn't say anything. Her eyes became shiny.

"Don't you and Dad care about our family?" I said. "Don't you guys care about me?"

"Of course we do," she said, smiling through a tear that ran down her left cheek. "That's not . . . "

"You've been better," I said. "You're not sleeping all the time anymore. You're cooking healthy meals for me again. What is Dad's problem?"

"Honey, your dad and I, we've grown apart. And it had nothing to do with you. Or whether we love you. It just happened."

"I don't understand."

"You will one day," she said. "But for right now, just know that both of us love you."

I stood up from the dining room table.

"No!" I said. "It didn't just happen! There has to be a reason. Tell me why!"

Now the tears really started coming down her face. I couldn't see her cry like that, so I bolted out of the dining room and up the stairs to my room. I shut the door and sat down on my bed. I looked to the far wall and saw my dad's Pistons jersey that he had given me when I was younger. It hung in a plastic display case over my desk. I ripped the case off the wall and smashed it on the side of my bed frame until it broke open, just enough that I could pull the jersey out of the plastic. I took the scissors out of the top drawer of my desk. I cut his jersey into pieces and threw them in my garbage can. I tossed the scissors onto my desk, and that's when I noticed that my breathing was out of control. The heavy breaths came fast, one right after the other, and then the dizziness hit. The room spun and I started to sweat. I dropped down into bed—on my back—until my breathing slowed to normal. The last thing I remembered before knocking out was that I was angry at both of my parents now. Angry and sad.

TWELVE

We had a light practice the next day after school because our first game of the season was the day after that. I didn't say one word to my dad on the ride to school that morning. And I didn't plan to. After practice, he met me outside the locker room and said that we needed to talk. I told him I didn't have anything to say, that he and my mom were the ones with explaining to do. He told me to follow him around to the side of school, where there were no people. I did so.

"About six months ago, I met another woman," he said.

I lunged at him with two balled up fists. I swung

them wildly trying to hurt him, but he was still too strong. He grabbed hold of me and tried to hug me while I continued thrashing. I got loose and took both fists and pushed them into his chest with all of my strength. He back slammed in the brick wall behind him and I stood where I was, eyes wide open. I tried to run away, but he sprang off the wall and grabbed me by the arm. He brought me in close, wrapped his arms around me, and whispered in my ear that everything was going to be okay. My eyes filled with water and I put my mouth into his ribcage to cover up the sound. He just kept his arms around me with one hand on the back and head, telling me over and over that we would get through this.

———

We were in the car now, heading home. I could see the hurt in my dad's eyes as he drove.

"Who is she?" I said, out of the blue, breaking the heavy silence between us.

"She's—"

"Why would you do that to mom?" I said. "What's so good about this woman?"

"We grew apart a long time ago, me and your mother," he said.

"I'm old enough, dad," I said. "Just tell me the truth."

"This woman is everything that your mother is not," he said. "She has drive. She's created her own path in life. But it's not your mother's fault. When we got married, things were perfect. I had just been drafted, we were young and in love and ready to start a family. I was ready to lay roots down here in Detroit. But to do that, sacrifices had to be made. Your mother sacrificed for me to chase my dream. *She* left Boston to come to Detroit with me. *She* stayed stay home with you, every day, when I was traded to Phoenix and while I was in Europe. And don't get me wrong, she wanted to be there with you, taking care of you day in and day out."

"So you being away had a lot to do with it?" I said.

"Yes, that was the start of our problems," he said, with a sad laugh. "I wasn't here in person long enough for us to fight in those days."

"All I remember from when you were in Europe was that I was always with mom," I said. "And that she was happy."

"She was," he said, "because she was with you. Underneath? Well, she held anger towards me. Before I got on the plane to Europe, she called me a hypocrite for ripping the family apart, the family that I had dreamed of."

I stayed silent. My dad never talked this much before. But the situation with our family wasn't this bad before.

"And when I retired and came back to Michigan full-time, things were good for a few years, remember?"

I nodded.

"But in the past two years or so, as you've

gotten busier with basketball, there's been less for your mother to do. She doesn't have that same *purpose* like when you were young. And when I'd tell her to try to look for a job or go back to school, I thought I was helping her. But really, I was pushing her away. She'd say that it's too late for her to do anything with her life and then I'd start insulting her and complaining nonstop. I said some things I truly regret. But those words can't be taken back, son."

He paused.

"That's when we'd have the bad fights."

"I never even noticed," I said.

"I'd drop you off at school in the morning and then come home, and we'd fight all day."

His eyes watered but no tears actually fell from his eyes.

"The truth is, I ruined it with your mother. I made her retreat like that. If you want to be mad at anybody, be mad at me. If you want to put the blame on someone, put it right here."

He pointed to his chest, right over his heart.

"Don't you ever think that she was a bad mother. Because it ain't the truth," he said.

I said nothing.

He was silent after that for a little while, too. We got into Auburn Hills. We passed by the same things we always did when we drove in from Detroit. But this day was different. There was a strange feel to it. We pulled up to the house and my dad cut the engine.

"Maybe if you come in," I said. "Apologize to mom for cheating on her. Then you could come back home, and maybe after a while things could get better. Like the way they were."

He sighed with his eyes still on the house that he paid for with all his hard work.

"There's too much hurt, Isaiah. That's why I could never live in the house again. I really believe that I—" he paused, "I ruined your mother's life. After her anger went away and she'd forgiven me for what I did, she said that she wanted me to come back home. I said no, and we agreed to get a divorce. I don't want to ruin your life by fighting all the time. You would've heard us going at it sooner or later. I can't put you through that."

I opened the door to get out and he put his hand on my arm.

"There's one more thing I need to tell you," he said.

I was ready for anything at that point. Whatever it was, I knew it would be bad.

"You're gonna have a baby sister."

———

"Mom!" I yelled when I walked into the house.

"Hi, Isaiah!" she said, from the kitchen. "Dinner is almost ready! Go wash your hands!"

When I walked through the front door, I stopped right in front of the stairs . I looked around the house like it was a foreign place. A place I didn't recognize. It was hard to hear my dad admit what he had done to my mom. To what he had done to me. And the worst part of it, the part that I couldn't get out of my head, was that he could just toss my mother and me away like trash, and start a new family.

I walked into the kitchen and the look on my face had to have been an awful one, because my mom realized right away that something was wrong. And the smile of her face quickly changed into a look of concern.

"What's the matter?"

"Dad told me . . . everything," I said.

"Everything?"

"I never want to see him again," I said. "For the rest of my life. From now on, I want you to take me to school. I want you to pick me up from practice and games. I'm done with him."

"Isaiah—"

"He ruined everything," I yelled. "He started a new family!"

The words jumped out of my mouth and I still

couldn't believe that they were true. My mom stood there, frozen. Her eyes were stuck on me and, for a moment, I wasn't sure if she knew what I was talking about.

"You know, right?" I said.

"Yes."

There was a long pause. She turned around and went back to cooking dinner.

"Go wash your hands," she said with her back to me.

I stood there for a minute, unable to move. She looked over her shoulder at me and then back to the food.

"It's better this way," she said. "It will be hard at first, but you'll see. It's better this way."

THIRTEEN

My dad wasn't in the stands for the first game of the season. The night before, I told my mom to call and tell him that I did not want him there.

I wasn't nervous at all for the game. Sure, it was the first game of the season. I was a freshman, named the starting point guard, and one of two captains for the team. Still, none of it fazed me. My workouts had prepared me for anything on the court.

I looked forward to being on the court, actually, to take my mind off what was going on at home.

We were playing against a public school from

Detroit without a strong basketball tradition. It would be an easy game for us. The bigger challenge was to start building chemistry. We were a young team as it was; losing Sherrod only made the task more difficult.

I walked into the locker room a couple of hours before the game and sat down next to Derrick. As team captains, our lockers were in the front, and right next to each other. I didn't say anything to any of my teammates as I passed. Just nods and fists pounds. I was focused on what I needed to do in the game, on what I needed to do for my team, but also pissed off about what was going on with my family.

Derrick looked to me and nodded as he pulled his socks on.

"What's up?" he said. "You good?"

"Fine," I said.

"You don't look it," he said.

I stood up and went to the trainers' room to get my ankles taped. As I walked by Dorrell at his locker, he looked up at me as if he were expecting me to say something. And his eyes were soft.

After getting taped up, Coach called me into his office.

I sat down in front of him at his desk.

"Everything okay?"

"It's fine," I said.

"Your father called this morning, said that he wouldn't be at tonight's game," he said. "And that he might not be at the games for a while."

I didn't say anything. I just stared back at him.

"Do you need someone to talk to?"

I took a deep breath and could feel the tears start to well up in my eyes. I held them back though. I shook my head.

"No more talking," I said. "I need to take this frustration out on somebody. I need to get out there on that court."

"All right," he said, seemingly satisfied with my answer. "I feel sorry for the other team tonight," he smiled.

That made me crack a little smile, too.

"Speaking of frustration," he said. "I had a talk with Dorrell. He's not going to be giving you any problems from now on. If he does, he'll be off the team."

"You didn't have to do that, Coach."

"We need to stick together right now. Can't have any of that stuff in this locker room."

"I'm gonna get some shots up, Coach."

I stood up to leave his office.

"Isaiah, wait."

I turned around to face him.

"This is your team now," he said. "With Sherrod gone, this is your show."

I nodded and walked out of his office, through the locker room and onto the court. The stands were empty now, as I went through my pregame shooting routine. The same routine my dad showed me when I was ten years old.

———

We started out the game on fire. We jumped them right from the opening tip, taking a fifteen to three lead in the first four minutes. As expected, they couldn't handle my speed or relentlessness. It didn't matter who they tried to guard me with. I blew past them all, either finding an open teammate for the score or taking it all the way to the hoop myself.

After one quarter, we were up thirty to sixteen and Coach took all the starters out for the beginning of the second quarter.

While I was on the bench, I looked up into the stands and found my mom a few rows up. She caught my glance and smiled. It was so weird not seeing my dad up there. But I could get used to it if I had to. What I couldn't get past yet was the anger. It was still there, lighting a fire inside of me.

When the starters came back in with four minutes left in the half, our lead was cut to nine. The first time I got the ball, I had my defender at the top of the key, right below the three point line. I yanked him with a wicked cross from right to left and he lost his feet for a moment. I elevated for the jumper and as he recovered, he clipped my side. I hit the floor. The shot splashed through the net and the whistle blew. Our crowd went crazy. I stared at the defender whom I had just embarrassed—his number was twenty-one. I started talking to him, "Come on, 21—you can't guard me."

He bumped me and got close.

"Keep talkin' shit," he said. "Little bitch-ass punk from the suburbs. Come see me outside after the game and we'll see what's up."

I stared back at him. "Shut the fuck up," I muttered.

Our teammates got between us and the referees warned us both.

I knocked down the free throw and bumped the lead back to twelve.

Trash talking was a part of the game. I was

used to the taunts about my height and where I lived. Most times I'd ignored them. On this night, though, I was out to prove a point. And I wasn't gonna take shit from anybody.

Right before halftime, with us up by seventeen, they had the ball. Number 21 dribbled on the left wing. He attacked, and when he tried to come with a weak-ass crossover, I took the ball from him and raced the other way. He gave chase but I blew right past him. As I got closer to our basket, I slowed down a bit. When I went up for the layup on the left hand side of the rim, Number 21 went for the block and smacked me across the head instead. All I heard as I fell to the floor was the crowd groan. I sprang up on my feet and turned around to look at him. I knew then that the foul was intentional, just by the look in his eye. The refs bolted over to us to keep the peace, but they couldn't hold me back. I went after him and grabbed his jersey with both hands. He grabbed hold of me, too, and by the time we finished pushing and pulling, we were all the way against the wall underneath the basket.

A mob of people followed us there. All of our teammates, plus the coaches and referees, were on that part of the floor. It seemed like all of the air in that entire gym was being sucked out. It was hard to get a breath. But it didn't matter. I wouldn't let go of his collar. It didn't matter how many people there were trying to pull me off.

Somewhere in the rush of it, I looked up briefly to the stands. My mother wasn't in her seat, she was closer to the court now, with a horrified look on her face. She yelled something to me. I could see her, but it was no use trying to hear what she said. There was too much chaos around. Too many bodies around me. She tried to get onto the floor, but there were security guards there to prevent her and others from storming the court.

I let go of Number 21 after that.

He smiled in my face.

"You ain't real, son," he said. "You a fake-ass tough guy."

That's when I punched him in the face with my left hand. My shooting hand. One of the first things my father ever taught me about basketball was to take care of my hands because, "They are what you use to do your job. You can't play the game with your hands." But here I was, risking the use of my hand—my shooting hand—to punch this clown that was talking smack. And my dad was nowhere to be found.

———

"You'll be suspended," Coach said, in his office after the game. "There's no doubt about *that*."

I was still in my uniform while Coach and I talked. The rest of the guys were long showered, changed, and on their way home. After I was thrown out of the game, we dominated the second half, winning by twenty-five points. I couldn't face my teammates after the game. I waited in the weight room while they cleared out.

"How long?" I said. "How many games do you think I'll be suspended for?"

"No idea," he said. "It'll probably be awhile. Maybe the whole season. I don't know. You threw a punch. The benches cleared. I have to talk to the commissioner tomorrow and let him know that the other player was baiting you. And that it had started earlier in the game. Maybe they'll take that into consideration."

I was still angry. Angry at Number 21. Angry at my dad. Angry at myself. Angry at the whole damn world.

"You gotta let this petty stuff go, Isaiah. About where you live," he said. "It's gonna cost you. But most of all, it's gonna cost the team. You're a captain, son. I don't know what else to say."

"I—"

He lifted his hand to quiet me down.

"It didn't cost us tonight, but it will. You don't

think when this gets out, that other teams are gonna try this with you? You just put a target on your chest."

I didn't reply. I put my head down. He was right, and I couldn't look him in the eye. I was failing as a leader, and also at providing hope for my team. I wasn't living up to any of the goals that I had set after Sherrod died.

"You have to grow up," he said. "None of that stuff matters. Whether you're from Detroit or Auburn Hills. None of that matters when you step on the court."

I raised my head back up and my eyes met his. "Okay, Coach."

"We play Mercy in two weeks. We can beat all the teams we play in the next two weeks without you. It'll be hard, but we can do it. We can't beat Mercy without you."

"Will I be suspended from school?"

"I'll let you know tomorrow," he said. "Go," he said. "Get changed. Take a shower. Cool down."

I nodded.

"Come see me after school tomorrow," he said. "I'll know something by then."

———

"That was awful," my mom said in the car as she took the 75 north exit toward Auburn Hills.

Those were the first words she spoke to me. Up until then, the car was quiet. I knew she was upset.

"I'm disappointed in you," she continued. "Disappointed, and embarrassed."

I didn't say anything because she was right.

"Your father is going to be upset when he hears about this," she said. "You're putting your future in jeopardy. And for what? Because someone is talking to trash to you?"

I still didn't say anything because I was tired of defending myself. It was hard to explain why I felt the way I did when someone questioned my toughness. It was a chip on my shoulder. And I didn't know how to get rid of it. That chip seemed to be getting bigger with Dad out of the picture.

"I'm gonna call him tomorrow and tell him what happened."

"He'll probably want to see me after," I said. "To talk about it."

"And you have to talk to him," she said. "I don't care how angry you are at him. This is your future, Isaiah. Your father has been through this. He can help you."

"What do you mean, he's been through this?" I said. "Dad grew up in the projects."

"You don't think there was racism where we grew up in Boston?" she said. "There were all kinds of people in our neighborhood. Not just blacks."

I looked at her as she spoke.

"He dealt with people calling him names, and even physical violence," she said. "But he found a way to use it to his advantage. And not let it destroy him."

"Do you know how he did it?" I said.

"He'll have to tell you," she said. "This is a lesson you need to learn from your father."

FOURTEEN

When I spoke to Coach the next day after school, he said that I would be suspended for the next two weeks. Just in time to play in the Mercy game. The commissioner went easy on me because of Sherrod. This was *big* because Mercy was the team that we defeated in the city championship the year before. They were going to be looking for revenge.

Luckily, I would not be suspended from school.

Coach stood up for me in his conversation with the commissioner. The deal Coach made came with a stern warning, and a new rule for the season. If anyone on our team fought during a game—no matter what the circumstances—they'd be out for the season. And that was that. The commissioner also told Coach that he would be monitoring our games going forward to make sure I wasn't being targeted by opposing teams.

My dad was supposed to pick me up after school to talk about what happened during the game. I did not want to hear what he had to say about his new family, or my mom and me—his old one. I just wanted it to be about basketball.

He pulled up in the Mercedes after school and I got in.

"Hey, son," he said.

"Hey, Dad."

"Want to talk about the game?"

I shrugged my shoulders.

"What happened?"

"Everything was good at first, I was doing my thing out there," I said. "And then this one guy starts talking. And then I start talking back."

"And?"

"Right before halftime, I got the steal and I'm

going to finish the layup and he just clocks me right in the back of the head," I said. "And I have to protect myself, right? That's what you always told me."

"Of course."

"But then, when we're getting into it, the guy says something to me and I just lost it."

"I heard you gave him a left hook to the face," he said, with a bit of pride.

"That's it," I said.

"How long are you suspended?"

I held up two fingers.

"Mercy game?"

"I'll be back in time for *that* game."

"What did the guy say to you? To cause you to lose it?"

"He said what all the rest of them say. He *basically* said that I'm not black enough."

"And if you're used to it by now, why did you lose control?"

"I don't know. I was excited about the game and

everything. But there was also this other feeling I had. Something that didn't feel good. With all the stuff that's been going on, I just haven't felt like myself."

My dad's shoulders slumped. He looked over to me and I saw the guilt in his eyes. And that hurt me. I didn't want to be angry at him, but I felt betrayed. It was almost too much to handle being in his car again, and it confused me. On one hand, it felt normal and gave me a feeling that maybe we could get over this and be a family again—a different kind of family. Still, the mistrust I felt towards him was strong. I didn't trust him at the moment. For betraying me. For betraying my mom. I wasn't sure if I could ever trust him again.

"Anyways," I said. "Mom thinks you can help me. That you've been through something like this before."

He took the exit towards Auburn Hills, keeping his eyes on the road.

"I raised you in Auburn Hills because I wanted

to protect you from the kinds of things I grew up with."

"It's giving me trouble, though," I said. "These guys from the city are gonna keep testing me. And I need to find a way to not react."

"I had the same problem as you, Isaiah," he said. "Except just in reverse. Some of the kids I grew up with didn't like blacks. They thought that we were in *their* neighborhood and that we were the ones who should leave."

I didn't say anything. I knew a story was coming. I could just tell by the look in his eyes. I didn't mind either. I liked his stories about his days growing up in Boston.

"When I was young, I used to think that you had to be pissed off when you stepped on the court," he said. "But one day back in Boston, I learned that it wasn't true. I was wrong. I never told you this story before. There was this older Irish kid named Tommy out on the playground who used to always pick on me during the games. He'd call me names, hack me every time I had the ball. Things like that. It almost got to the point where I was ready to quit playing basketball, just so I didn't have to see him anymore. I didn't quit though. And one day, during a game, Tommy called me a 'dumb nigger' and the next time we were down the floor, I popped him right in the side of the head with an elbow. It came out of nowhere. He wasn't ready for it and it knocked him flat on his back. I got on top of him and punched him in the face until both of us were covered in his blood. He begged me to stop hitting him and I wouldn't until *I* was done. None of the other kids on the court did anything. They just stood there staring at me."

His hands tensed up around the steering wheel as he told the story.

"Finally, I stopped hitting him," he said. "I ran home from the park and threw the bloody clothes away."

"What happened next?" I said. "How did you learn that you didn't have to be mad to play the game?"

"A few days later, we were all out on the playground and here comes Tommy," he said. "I thought that he was coming for revenge. But when it was his turn to play and he stepped on the court, he couldn't even look me in the eye anymore. He was so afraid of me. And it made me feel awful. I didn't want that. I wasn't angry about being black. I just got tired of taking shit for being black."

"Did he say anything to you?" I said. "Tommy?"

"No," he said. "But I said something. Before the game started, I walked over to him and shook his hand. I apologized for what I did and he accepted. We were fine after that. We even started playing on the same team during some of the games. And that never happened at the beginning."

He took the exit for Auburn Hills.

"From that moment on, I tried to be calm out on the court," he said. "It's hard. But it can be done."

He turned onto our street and pulled up right next to the house. *His* old house.

"Use this time away from the team to get your mind right," he said. "It's okay to stand up for yourself. I'm not saying that you should be a coward or anything like that. But just realize that when you retaliate, especially with violence—," he shook his head, "—it's gonna end up hurting you more."

I shook my head and put my hand on the door handle.

He put his hand on my shoulder.

"Son, I know you got upset about what I told you last time we saw each other—"

I opened the car door and got out. I started down the walkway that led to the front door.

He got out of the car too and I heard his footsteps follow me and then stop.

"Isaiah!" he said. "You turn around when I'm talking to you!"

I turned around slowly and faced him.

"I'm still your father," he said. "No matter what."

"I need some more time," I said. "To get my mind right. Honestly, I can't talk about this with you. Not yet. Come to the Mercy game. I'll be ready to see you up in the stands again by then."

FIFTEEN

My two weeks away from the team started on that Saturday. I wasn't allowed to practice with the team or even go to the games during that time. I was cut off completely.

With the weekend off, I had to decide what I was going to do with myself. There was a lot in my head. Too much. I thought about what the word "community" meant to me. How my actions could hurt my community. And how I wasn't living up to my third goal of getting out into the community and doing some good.

I wanted to change that.

"I want to go into the city," I said.

My mom and I were sitting down at the dining room table, having breakfast.

"You know you can't play with your team, Isaiah."

"I don't wanna watch the game," I said. "I want to volunteer somewhere. Maybe a homeless shelter. I don't know."

"That's . . . " she said. "That's a really good idea."

My mom helped me look up some of the shelters around Detroit. But you had to be eighteen years old to volunteer at most of them. The last option was the Y in South Detroit.

I dialed the number and handed the phone to her.

"Okay, you can volunteer at the Y," she said, hanging up the phone. "They allow volunteers under the age of eighteen, as long as the parent gives permission. They are expecting us for an event that they are having today."

"Us?"

"Yes, don't you want me to come?"

"I was kind of thinking that I could do this alone, Mom."

"Alone?" she said. "Why?"

"I just want to do this by myself," I said.

"Will you be okay, by yourself?"

"I'll be fine," I said.

She thought about it for a little while. A smile crawled across her face.

"Okay," she said. "Go get changed and I'll take you over there."

"Thanks, Mom."

I got up and gave her a kiss on the cheek before running upstairs to change.

——

We arrived at the Y in South Detroit about thirty minutes later. It was close to the party house that I went to with Derrick and Tishaun. The weather was perfect considering that it was winter. The sun was shining and there was no chill in the air.

We got out of the car and walked over to an older woman with a clipboard in her hand.

"Hello," I said. "I'm here to volunteer for the event."

"Oh, hello baby," she said. "How old are you?"

"Fourteen."

"Is that your mother?" she said, pointing behind me.

I nodded.

My mom signed a sheet of paper that allowed me to volunteer. I walked over to the car with her and she got in the driver's side and rolled down the window.

"Are you sure you don't want me to stay?"

"I'll be fine, Mom."

"What time should I pick you up?"

"I'm going to take the bus back."

"What are you talking about?" she said. "I'll come pick you up."

"I want to."

"Isaiah, I know your suspension from the team is a big deal, but I think you're going a little too far with this. Volunteering is good enough. It's a good start."

"Just let me do this, Mom," I said.

"Do you have money for the bus?" she said. "Do you even know which bus gets you to Auburn Hills?"

"I'll find out from one of these nice people here," I said, smiling.

She looked around at all the other volunteers and staff members setting up for the event.

"Okay," she said, jabbing at me with her pointer finger. "You call me if you need me. And don't stay too late."

"I have my cell phone, Mom."

"Bye, honey," she said, before starting the car.

"Bye, Mom."

She pulled away from the Y and there I was,

alone again in the city. This time, under totally different circumstances

I walked over to the older woman with the clipboard.

"What's happening today?" I said.

"We're having our monthly donation drive," she said. "There's also going to be free food, sports clinics, and health classes for the public."

My eyes lit up when she said the word "sports."

"You like sports?"

I smirked, hoping she didn't take it as disrespect.

"Yes, I do. Especially hoops."

"Okay," she said. "Let's get you a volunteer badge."

———

The woman with the clipboard went by the name of Gloria. She quickly introduced me to many of the workers and put me to work just as fast. My first job was to help with a basketball clinic for ten-year-old kids from South Detroit. We put them through drills and showed them some basic ways they could practice and improve. I remembered being that age and already being on organized teams in Auburn Hills. Even back then, I was well on my way to developing the skills that I was now using on the court. For many of the kids that I worked with that day, it was the first time they had even touched a basketball. I noticed that whenever you told them something or tried to instruct them, there was very little eye contact in return. By the end of the clinic, I told the kids that when someone is trying to teach you something, it's best to look at their face, just like I had learned.

After we were done with the clinic, I was moved to lunch duty, where I helped serve the food provided by a local restaurant. I greeted people as they sat down at their tables, taking their drink and food orders next, and serving the food at the table when it was time. This was a lot of fun. Talking to people and actually getting a chance to interact with them. The people at the tables were as diverse as the food on the menu. Some were black. Some were white.

After the first rush, Gloria came over and put her hand on my back.

"You take a break, baby," she said. "You've deserve it."

"Can I ask you a question?" I said in a low voice. "Is everyone here homeless?"

She smiled.

"No," she said. "Some, but not all. Some are working poor. Lookin' for a good meal when money is tight."

I nodded and looked around at the tables filled with people who were just trying to get a meal. It made me feel small to be upset about a stupid comment made on a basketball court. Even the stuff with my Dad started to feel unimportant.

"I really like that we get to serve people," I said.

She patted me on the back again.

"There's more dignity that way," she said. "Excuse me, baby."

She went to go talk to another volunteer.

I got a plate of food for myself and found an empty seat at a table where a family was sitting. We didn't talk, just exchanged smiles instead while enjoying an unseasonably warm day in Detroit.

———

After the event was finished, all of the volunteers helped with the cleanup. It took about two hours to finish, and after that, Gloria gathered up the entire group of volunteers.

"I just want to say thank you to all of you, from the whole staff of the South Detroit Y," she said. "You all don't know how much this means to the community. And we thank God for people like you. We ask God every day for more people like you."

Gloria started clapping.

"Thank you."

Next thing I knew, all of the volunteers were clapping and it felt like I was a part of a team again. It was really cool.

I walked over and gave Gloria a hug and told her that whenever my schedule allowed it, I'd be down there to help at more events.

It was four in the afternoon now. The sun would be out for another hour or so. My team was just getting ready to play their first game without me. I wasn't ready to go back to Auburn Hills yet. I didn't want to go home and have nothing to do. There would be too much time to dwell on my suspension.

I felt like walking around some.

"Miss Gloria!" I called out.

"Yes?"

"How do I get downtown from here?" I said. "With the bus."

"You take the Eight Mile. It's right over there,"

she said, as she pointed at the bus stop across the street. "And get off at Congress Street."

"Thanks."

"If you hurry, there's one coming in three minutes."

"Okay. Bye!"

"Bye, baby."

I ran over to the bus stop and Gloria was right. The Eight Mile came in three minutes. I waved to her across the street before boarding the bus.

I took a seat at the back of the almost empty bus. One of the first stops was in front of Sherrod's building. I remembered what it looked like from the day my dad took me to it. At the last second, I pulled the cord and hopped off the bus. I walked over to the building. There weren't many people out and the sun was starting to go down, taking the warm weather with it. There were three guys though—looked like they were in their late teens— hanging out near the spot where Sherrod was killed. They were laughing and talking, each one with a brown paper bag in his hand. I tried not to look like a visitor—there to observe and judge—but failed. I couldn't help but stare at the spot where Sherrod died.

"You need some help?" one of them said.

"Nah," I said.

"Whatchu looking at, then?" another one said.

"I'm just . . . "

"You know a boy got shot here?" the first one said.

"Yeah," I said. "Sherrod. I knew him."

This got their attention. Their eyes narrowed.

"What you mean? Knew him?" the first one said.

"We played ball on the same team."

They relaxed, and then I was able to relax.

"Well, walk on then," the first one said, taking a sip from the can in his paper bag and looking past me. "Ain't nothing to see here."

I nodded and walked away.

They didn't even think twice about standing on that spot. They didn't worry about bad luck or anything like that. People got shot in their neighborhood all the time. Luck had nothing to do with it.

I waited for the next Eight Mile and it took ten minutes to show up. I got on and continued my trip downtown. The bus made a lot of stops while we were still in South Detroit and it filled up quickly. When we turned onto Eight Mile Road, two guys who looked like they were in their early twenties, got on and walked to the back of the bus. They sat down across from me.

One of them looked familiar and the other didn't.

The familiar looking one caught me glancing at him.

"Yo, you play ball, right?"

"Yeah," I said.

"You play for DCD?"

That stood for Detroit County Day School, the middle school I had attended.

"Yeah," I said. "Did you play there?"

"Nah," he said. "I went to Emerson."

I couldn't figure out where it was I knew him from. I just knew that I recognized his face.

He snapped his fingers.

"I was your counselor from a couple summers ago," he said. "UDM summer camp."

The University of Detroit-Mercy basketball camp was one of the most popular camps in the area, more so than MU or Michigan State's. And the reason was because UDM is in the city; any kid from Detroit who was interested in the camp was allowed free admission to the day sessions. All the best players from the area attended—no matter their age—and famous players in the area always came back to speak. In the past, my dad was a speaker at the camp, and Isaiah Thomas and Jalen Rose were the speakers the years that I attended.

"Oh yeah!" I said.

"You were an overnight camper, right?" he said.

"That's right.

"What's your name?"

"Isaiah."

"Your dad played for the Pistons, right?"

"Yeah."

"I remember you now," he said. "You had the jets and the nice handles."

"That's me."

"Where do you play now?"

"Detroit Catholic."

"You gotta be what, a sophomore by now?"

"Freshman."

"JV?"

I shook my head, "varsity."

"Freshman playing varsity?" he said and then turned to his friend. "I knew this kid was going to be nice."

There was another pause as he thought for a moment.

"Don't you guys have a game tonight?" he said.

Now it was my turn to think. He obviously knew that Saturday night was a big night for high school basketball in Detroit. There was no use in lying.

"I'm suspended," I said. "I got into a fight last game."

"Did he talk about your mama?" he said, with a smile.

"Nah, it was stupid."

"What are you doing on this side of town?" he said. "Your school is north side."

"I'm not really sure."

"You live in the city?"

"No. I live in Auburn Hills."

His friend pulled the cord to get off at the next stop.

"Aight, Isaiah," he said, as he and his friend stood up to leave. "Keep giving them hell on the court. Just make sure that you can actually *be* on the court."

We shook hands and they walked towards the door.

"Yo!" I said. "What's your name again?"

"Kevin," he said.

"Where are you playing at these days?"

"I don't play anymore," Kevin said. "I coach. South Detroit Youth League."

Kevin exited the bus and the doors clapped shut.

———

By the time the bus stopped at Congress Street, the city was dark. The streets were deserted. I got off the bus and stared straight up into the air, straining my neck to see where the skyscrapers ended and the dark sky began.

It was no use.

The emptiness didn't make sense.

Where was everyone?

I walked a couple more blocks and still didn't see another person. I looked up to the sky again and the buildings in the distance caught my gaze. It was so quiet that I thought I could hear the Detroit River flowing, even though I was many blocks away from it. But I was fooled. It was just a trick my mind was playing.

I remembered when I was a young boy, looking at the skyline of Detroit from the car and thinking it was a magical place. It had always been that for me. A place where I came to live out my dreams. I related the city to playing ball, and the empty feeling I had standing there in a deserted city gave my stomach a turn. It couldn't be further than the feeling of joy I had experienced playing ball in the city all those years.

I wasn't standing in the Detroit that I knew. I was standing in some foreign place. With no one around. No one to ask directions from.

The air turned cold in what seemed like an instant. I put my hands in my pockets and huddled in the doorway of a skyscraper to take cover from the wind that was nonexistent earlier in the day.

The gusts died down, allowing me to continue my walk. I turned around to look up at the skyscraper. Like the streets surrounding it, the skyscraper was also empty. I backed away from it and started running. I ran as fast as I could away from that empty building, worried that its bad luck would rub off on me and shatter my dreams. My chest burned as the cold air jabbed holes into it. My mouth and nose dried up. Suddenly, I couldn't get any air.

I didn't want to call my parents. I had to understand what was happening on my own.

The silence of the streets offered no answers, but said a lot at the same time.

I got to the end of a block and it seemed like it was the end of the city.

It was time to leave. The sky was black and I could smell snow in the air. I finally found another person, a cop, and asked him how I could get back to Auburn Hills. He chuckled and asked me how someone could be that lost. The only response that I could give back to him was a shoulder shrug. I got into his car and he dropped me off at the stop for the first of three buses I had to catch back to Auburn Hills.

My life had changed so much in the span of a

couple of weeks. I had a feeling that it would keep changing. And that if I wasn't willing to go along with the changes, I'd lose it all and be left empty, just like the city. Detroit.

I watched the empty skyscrapers against the dark sky as they rushed away through the window of a bus on the 75 north. I had to pay close attention. The city moved away far and fast, until it was so distant, so absent, that it slipped my mind altogether.

SIXTEEN

The team didn't lose any games during my suspension, going a perfect 6-0 over the two week span. None of the games were close, which wasn't a surprise. But that did nothing to heal my damaged ego. I now knew that the team didn't need me to be successful. It was the other way around. I needed them.

I also didn't spend any more time with Dad over that period, choosing instead to spend a bunch of time with my mom, in an effort to strengthen our weakened bond. He called a few times to ask if I wanted to work out or go grab a burger, but I told him that we were going to stick to the night of the

Mercy game for us to see each other next. The fact that my dad left us for another family still stung—a lot. And I wasn't sure how much time it would take go away. My mom told me to be patient and that with more time, it would get better, and then when I was ready—if I'd ever be ready—we could have a relationship again.

One day I asked her if she would ever forgive him and she told me that she would answer my question honestly. She said that, like me, she wasn't sure if she could forgive him. I appreciated her honesty. It was a sign that I was becoming more mature, and that I could handle the truth.

Truth is though, I wasn't sure if I wanted that or not. I didn't know if our relationship would ever be the same. A lot had happened since the beginning of the season, Sherrod's death being the biggest and most important. But as far as the situation with my parents was concerned, this much was true: I knew I still loved both of them. There was no question about that. And I knew they both loved me, too.

I had a big decision to make. Either I had to try to forgive, try to have a relationship with him—a different kind, no doubt—or I had to truly decide that I couldn't be around him anymore. Maybe what he did to my mom and I was too awful to come back from.

The night before the Mercy game was the last night of my suspension. I would be eligible to play in the game on the following night. It would be hard coming in rusty against *that* team. But I had no other choice. Playing it safe and coming back from suspension against an easier opponent was not an option. And I had a lot to prove to a lot of people. I had to prove to my coach and teammates that I could be the one to lead them after the tragedy of Sherrod's murder. I had to prove to my dad that I had learned enough from him to go on and be successful. And I had to prove to myself that I had grown. Winning the Mercy game would be the proof I needed.

I picked up the phone and dialed my dad's cell phone before I went to bed that night.

"Hello?" he said. "Janet?"

"No, it's me."

"Isaiah?"

"Yeah."

"What's up, son?"

"Just wanted to make sure that you're going to be at the game tomorrow."

"Of course," he said, before there was a silence over the line. "You want me there, right?"

"Yeah."

"I'll be there. You know I wouldn't miss any of your . . . you know if the situation was—"

"One other thing."

"Yes, son?"

"Don't bring anybody else," I said. "Come alone. And I want you to sit by mom."

There was more silence.

"Okay, son," he said. "Okay."

SEVENTEEN

First thing in the morning on the day of the Mercy game, Coach called me into his office. Even though I was at school attending classes during the full two week suspension, I wasn't allowed to have any contact with him.

"Glad to see that you're still in shape," he said, with a smile.

"I got some work in over my . . . break."

"With your dad?"

"No, I found another gym to get my work in," I said. "In Auburn Hills."

"Will he be up in the stands tonight?"

I nodded.

Coach held up a sheet of paper in front of his face and then peeked his eyes over it.

"What's that?" I said.

He slapped the sheet down on his desk.

"It's a memo from the commissioner's office, saying that the refs are going to be watching you closely tonight. They're gonna make sure that Mercy's players are behaving. And also that the same goes for you."

I nodded.

"Keep your head in the game," he said. "Focus is your biggest objective for tonight."

"I'm focused, coach."

"Good," he said. "Now get to class."

I got up and started to leave the office. But before I walked out of it, one last thing came to mind.

"Coach," I said, by the doorway.

He looked up at me.

"I can play the whole game if you need to me to."

He just smiled.

"You know, make up for lost time."

This was the biggest game in my life up to that point. Mercy didn't care that we had lost Sherrod—our best player from the year before—to murder. They didn't care that my family had fallen apart. There would be no sympathy from anyone.

On that night, Sherrod's name would be remembered one way or another. My school was planning to retire his jersey at halftime. His name and number would go up there in the rafters with some of Detroit's finest. It was on me to make sure that Sherrod's jersey would go up on the night of a win.

———

Coach went over the game plan with us in the locker room after school, focusing a lot of attention on the details of our defensive strategy. This was the first time I had seen the game plan and it took me a little while to understand the wrinkles that Coach had put in during my absence.

"So you see," Coach said to me in the center of the locker room, "I want you to go under all of the pick and rolls when their point guard has the ball. Just let him shoot all night. We can live with that."

Mercy was a tall team. They had a big height advantage over us and we knew they would use it. As we watched cut-ups from all of their earlier games that season, it was clear that their plan would be to pound the ball inside to soften us up early, and then use that to key their outside game late.

Coach wanted aggressive double-teams on their two big men. But with that kind of defense, the rotations had to be tight. We went through each rotation over and over, until there was no more time to do so.

And after showing us the final defensive rotation, Coach smiled and turned the video projector off.

"Okay, take all that stuff that I just told you, all those X's and O's, and just forget 'em. Forget it all. I want you guys out there playing fast. Don't be out there thinking too much."

He pointed to his head.

"If the stuff sticks up here, great. If not, just make sure you're playing with your hair on fire."

The room was silent.

We were ready.

I was ready.

"Okay, let's do this," he said.

———

We all knew that we would need to focus to beat Mercy. There was the revenge aspect of it: Mercy was a veteran team compared to us and wanted nothing better than to beat us on our home floor. Doing so would provide a little bit of payback for beating them in the championship game last year, while also claiming the inside track to the playoffs for that season.

Instead of sitting next to Derrick in the locker room before the game, I switched it up. I found

Dorrell sitting at the end of a bench. There was an open seat directly across from him.

I walked down to where he was.

I nodded to the open seat, across from him.

"Is that seat taken?"

He looked up at me and I noticed a little bit of surprise in his eyes.

He shrugged his shoulders.

"Free country," he said.

We sat together in silence, but we were together. Some guys played cards. Some listened to music. Dorrell and I started to chat, running through assignments for the game. I had asked him to go over the defensive game plan again with me, and he was cool enough to help without making a big deal about it.

"You gotta look out for the lob to one of their big men whenever they grab an offensive board," he said, pointing down to the call sheet. "They always try to go quick when they get another possession."

"Cool," I said.

"That's all of it," he said. "You should be good."

"Hey Dorrell," I said. "Thanks for holding things down while I was out."

"Well, you back now," he said. "Hopefully, you don't go punching nobody tonight."

"I won't," I said. "Sorry I was a punk."

We shook hands.

"I got you," he said. "Just do your thing out there tonight."

With just twenty minutes to go before tip, I needed a moment to clear my head. I sat in a bathroom stall alone, taking a moment to think about all that happened since the season started.

I thought about my dad and his demanding ways. I remembered the first time he ever fouled me hard on a basketball court. I was eight and he was home for the holidays from Europe. He knocked me on my ass while I was driving to the hoop. It wasn't a hard shot, but it caught me off guard. He helped me up, and after wiping my tears away and rubbing the bruise on my elbow, he told me that getting knocked down wasn't what life was about. Getting up was "the thing."

Thoughts of Sherrod came to my head last.

We had a bond, even though we didn't get a fair chance to strengthen it.

I stretched out in the tiny stall. I prepared for not only a physical battle but also a mental one. I knew there would come a time in the game where one of their guys would try me. I had to rise above it somehow, no matter how difficult it was.

When I was done with my mental prep, I left the bathroom. That's when it hit me: I had to win the game for Sherrod. *We* had to win for him.

———

We waited in the locker room for Coach to give us his final speech.

The room was quiet. We could hear our crowd chanting the school song in the gym just a few steps away.

Coach walked in, his mouth tight and his eyes focused.

"You guys are something," he said. "All of you."

He paced a bit and then stopped.

"Forget about this game. Basketball doesn't mean a damn thing. There's real life out there. Out there on those streets. I want all of you to know that you have value. And I'm not talking about on the basketball court. You have value in the classroom. You have value in your communities. People look up to you in your neighborhoods. They say, 'Hey, maybe if I do it the right way, I can have a positive influence on the neighborhood.' You're all valuable. Every last one of you."

He paused for a second.

"And of course, there is one less of you than there should be. He was taken away from his neighborhood. Taken away from his school. Taken away from us. I can't understand why it happened. I'm still angry about it. But I can't do anything about it. So the message is—"

He put one finger in the air.

"You only get one go around in this life, men," he said. "Be valuable."

I looked around the locker room and didn't see one blink of an eye.

"Hair on fire, gentleman," he said. "Hair on fire."

We took the floor.

The scene in the gym was nothing like I had ever seen before. There was a buzz that I thought was only possible at the pro level. I saw the crowd as one wave of blue—our main color—with patches of red—Mercy's color—around the stands. I saw my parents at center court, three rows up. They were together just like I asked them to be. I smiled at them and they smiled back.

I walked over to the sideline and my mom blew a kiss. It was like the old days, when both of them would be in the stands cheering me on. My dad nodded to me and motioned that he wanted to come close. I nodded back. He walked down the three rows and one of the security guards allowed him to get on the sideline.

We shook hands and he gave me a big hug.

"You ready?" he yelled, over the chants of our home crowd.

I nodded.

"Get after them!" he said. "Surprise them with that speed. Take it to them."

I nodded again.

"I'm gonna win this game for Sherrod," I said, out of nowhere.

He smiled.

"Go play," he said.

He patted me on the back and walked back up into the stands.

Right before the game started, Coach pulled me aside.

"Mercy is a great team, they probably won't pull any of that bush-league bullshit. *But*, you never know," he said. "Focus."

He pointed to his head.

I nodded and Coach gave me a hug.

The first thing that stuck out about Mercy when we went out for the jump ball was their size. The film didn't lie. Even their guards were at least six-foot-four. And they were all strong too, with wide shoulders and bulging muscles. They looked like a football team on the basketball court. I knew it was going to be a long game just by looking at them. I was ready for it, though.

I shook hands with all their players one by one. Their point guard was last. He was four inches taller than me and probably thirty pounds heavier.

"Good luck out there, rook," he said.

I said the same, minus the "rook."

We won the tip, and on our first possession, I got into the lane and hit a right-handed floater. After getting a steal on their first possession, I pushed the ball down the floor and found Derrick in the corner for a wide-open three. We scored on our next two possessions and went up nine to two. Mercy called an early timeout. Our crowd erupted and I couldn't even hear myself think on the way back to the bench.

Coach didn't say anything about strategy in the huddle. It was way too early for adjustments. All he said, over and over, was: "Don't relax! They are going to come right back at you! Now it's your turn to withstand *their* punch!"

Coach was right. They did punch back. They hit us with a ten-O run to take a three-point lead with half the first quarter gone. They did it the way we expected them to. They force-fed the ball inside for two easy scores and when we brought double teams on their next two possessions, they kicked the ball out for open threes.

After a timeout of our own, I went on my own personal six-O run. Even though their point guard was bigger than me, he had trouble keeping up with me, either straight up or on the pick-and-roll. My last bucket of the run was sweet, a lefty floater that flew just over a shot-blocker's hand and kissed off the glass and in.

We traded buckets the rest of the way and it was twenty-three to twenty in our favor at the end of the first quarter.

Coach came to me on the bench.

"Do you need a blow?"

"I'm good," I said.

"I can steal you two minutes here if you need a rest!" he screamed.

"I'm good!" I said. "I'll tell you if I'm tired."

"Okay."

Mercy brought in some reserves at the beginning of the second quarter and we did too, giving us a lineup of three bench players along with Derrick and me.

I knew before the game that Coach couldn't afford to take Derrick and me out of the game for too many minutes, if any. My legs were fresh with the two weeks off. I was up for it. Derrick looked fine, too. I hoped that he hadn't been drinking and smoking since the season started back up.

We took advantage of their reserves for the

first four minutes of the quarter and opened up a ten-point lead. They couldn't stop Derrick and me from playing a slick, two-man game. And they *really* couldn't handle my speed. I capped the run with another steal and finished with a powerful one-handed dunk on the other end. My first dunk of the season—and it brought the crowd to their feet.

Mercy called another timeout and the gym was so loud my ears were popping. After the play, I looked to my parents' spot in the stands, watching closely for my dad's wide eyes in response to my slam. But it was no use. All I saw was blue.

Coach tried to take me out again during the timeout, but again, I refused.

Mercy brought their starters back in after the timeout and stormed back into the game. They did so by getting our big men in foul trouble and marching to the free throw line. They got our frontline into so much foul trouble that we had to let them score a few uncontested layups. Our bigs had to save their fouls for the second half because our bench was razor thin at the forward and center positions.

The game was tied with twenty seconds to go in the first half. I had it at mid-court, scanning the defense until I was ready to attack. At ten seconds to go, I broke my man down and got into the lane. I elevated for a layup on the left side and next thing I knew, I was clobbered. The shot was blocked into the stands, but the ref blew his whistle for the foul. The player who fouled me was their power forward, coming out of nowhere to protect the rim, and tattooing me in the process.

I landed hard, right on my left hip. I could hear the bone crunch against the hardwood. The worst part about it, though, was that the guy who fouled me landed right on top of me. It was like rubbing salt in a wound. I stayed on the floor for at least a minute to catch my wind. When they peeled me up off the floor, my whole left side was numb. I couldn't feel my left foot touching the floor. Their power forward who fouled me gave me a pat on the butt and asked me if I was okay.

I said "yeah" even though I wasn't. It was a clean foul. No dirt in it at all. It was just two guys getting after it, going full speed. Unfortunately for me, I was fifty pounds lighter than the guy who smashed into me and then landed on top of me.

I still didn't have full feeling in my limbs, but I had to shoot the free throws. The rules said that if I came out of the game for injury and didn't take my foul shots, I couldn't play in the second half. That was not an option.

I stepped to the free throw line and knocked down one of two. We took a one point lead into the locker room at halftime. The score was forty-nine to forty-eight. I had fourteen points, five assists, three rebounds and four steals. The rebounds always gave me the most pride, getting in there amongst the trees.

I needed a teammate's help getting back to the locker room. The bruise on my left hip had already started to swell. The trainer took hold of me once I got in there.

"It's a bone bruise," he said. "A bad one. But nothing's fractured."

Coach came into the trainers' room and closed the door. My teammates were quiet in the locker room, waiting for the next set of bad news in a season that had been filled with it up to that point.

Coach put his arm around my shoulder.

"Let's live to fight another day, Isaiah," he said. "Take a seat for tonight."

I gritted my teeth as the trainer rubbed my hip bone. It was raw to the touch.

"I'm not coming out of the game," I said through a wince. "Not *this* game."

Coach took a deep breath.

"If I leave you in the game," he said. "They'll attack you, Isaiah."

"As they should," I said.

And that was it. There was no more discussion.

Coach patted me on the back and left.

The trainer told me that the best he could do for me was to rub some cream on the bruise to try to numb it. I said that was fine. He said that there would still be significant pain. I told him that was fine, too.

The only adjustment that Coach made was to take me off the ball on offense. My speed would be affected because of the bum hip. There would be no blowing by guys in the second half. I had to be a finisher instead of a creator. He asked me if I thought I could hit shots and I told him yes. Derrick would handle the ball and I would stand on the weak side. This was a flip-flop of our usual roles when I was one hundred percent.

My first few steps on the floor were tentative. If walking was a challenge, I didn't even want to think what running would be like. I bit my lip hard and put the pain in my hip out of my head.

The second half started and they attacked me right off the bat. Their point guard took me down into the post and scored on two straight possessions.

Even if I was full strength, I would've had trouble with him down there. He was big and strong, not to mention experienced. A bad combination for me. I was glad that they didn't use that strategy earlier in the game.

Our offense was also flat to start the third quarter. Without my creativity and speed, our possessions slowed to a crawl and our spacing became terrible. I just stood in the corner, unable to cut to the basket because of the pain.

We fell behind by seven early in the quarter, before Coach called a timeout. Our crowd, which had been so vocal in the first half, was silenced. Only Mercy's small cheering section made noise now. Their school song rang out during the timeout.

"I'm taking you out," Coach said. "You gave it a shot."

"It's gonna loosen up, Coach," I pleaded. "Trust me."

I was not sure that it would loosen.

"I'm gonna give you three more minutes in this quarter."

Three minutes to prove myself. Three minutes to give myself a chance. Three minutes to have the chance to win the game for Sherrod.

Coach turned away from me and went into the huddle. I didn't join it, but could hear him screaming: "You guys have to move on offense! Stop standing around! And set some screens, god-dammit!"

On our first possession out of the timeout, I stood in the corner once again. Derrick took a horrible, highly-contested jumper. But instead of giving up on the play, on running back down on defense, I tried for the offensive rebound. To my surprise, I was able to elevate and out-jump their power forward for the board. I went right back up with the ball and hit a layup, plus the foul. Our crowd cheered after the whistle blew, begging us for more reasons to get excited.

Their power forward looked at me with shock.

The fact that I was the one who grabbed the rebound, the smallest guy on the floor with a bum hip, had taken him by surprise. His jaw was on the floor and his eyes were wide open. The play was huge for two reasons: first, it got us a needed score and second, it gave their power forward four fouls. The fifth would foul him out.

I hit the free throw and—*what do you know,* my hip loosened up. I was able to be more active on defense and when their point guard tried to post me up again, I used my speed to sneak around him and steal the entry pass.

I took control of the ball-handling duties again on offense and we scored on our next three possessions. I hit a floater on one possession and set up teammates for open jumpers on the other two.

I wasn't as fast as I normally was, but at seventy percent I was faster than most people.

The score was once again tied at sixty eight after three quarters.

In between quarters, our crowd was silent. They

must've sensed that it would be a tight game all the way to the end. They, too, were saving their energy for a big finish. Coach didn't say much to us in the huddle and he didn't say anything to me specifically. He knew I wasn't coming out of the game. And at that point in the game, what else was there to say? There were no more adjustments to make. It was just two teams going at each other with all they had. Coach couldn't help us out there on the floor. My dad couldn't help me out there on that floor. No one could. We held our own destiny.

The last period started with the two teams trading baskets for the first six possessions. Their strategy was to go back to pounding us down low, and our strategy was to use our speed to get buckets.

Strength versus strength.

On their fourth possession, I got switched onto a much taller player because of a back screen. The player pinned me underneath the basket, but when he turned to lay the ball in the hoop, I stripped him down low and stole the ball. The ref blew the whistle and called a horrible, terrible foul. I'd stripped him clean. Didn't get any of his hand.

I looked at the ref in disbelief.

"Are you kidding me?" I yelled.

Coach was yelling at him too, from the sideline as one of the other refs restrained him.

Our crowd booed the ref mercilessly and then quickly changed gears, coming with a chant that cursed his existence.

"You need to calm down, son!" the ref yelled back at me.

"How could you call that?" I said, with a wave of the hand.

The player that I stripped clean was at the free throw line to shoot two. I glanced at him and he responded with a guilty smirk. He knew they got away with one. I had to let it go, though. I had to focus. There was still plenty of time left in the game and I couldn't go in the tank.

He hit both of the free throws to put them up

two. I responded to the bad call by slashing to the hoop on a side-pick-and-roll, and hitting Derrick in the corner for an open three, which he nailed.

We stopped them on the next possession—Derrick got a steal—and on the other end, we set them up with the same, side-pick-and-roll action that they had trouble stopping the whole game.

They brought an aggressive double-team this time, and I split it. I found Derrick again for a corner three. He hit it again. But this time he was fouled as he let the ball fly. The ref—the same one that called the phantom foul on me—blew his whistle on Derrick's shot. Our crowd exploded one more time. It was the loudest outburst of the whole game. I thought the roof was going to come off the gym.

Derrick pumped his fist as he sat on the floor. He screamed, "Let's go!" at least five times. He knocked the free throw down for the four point play.

Mercy called a timeout to regroup. There were

three minutes left in the game and we had a four point lead.

I was exhausted. So exhausted that I didn't even realize how exhausted I was. My whole body was numb now. I didn't want to sit down on the bench for fear of my legs locking up. The crowd was chanting our school song once again. It seemed to get louder and louder as the timeout wore on, to the point where the sound became suffocating. I tried to block all the noise out of my head. It was difficult but, I succeeded. Sherrod came to my thoughts at that moment for some reason. I didn't put his memory out of my mind. I left him in my thoughts. I didn't have the energy to block out thoughts and finish the game all at the same time.

The ref blew his whistle and both teams went back out on the floor. Mercy scored on their next two possessions to tie the game up at eighty-two. Derrick turned the ball over on our next possession and they took their time on offense to kill some of the clock. Their point guard took me down in the post and I didn't have any legs left to fight him off. I tried to poke the ball out of his hands with a reach-in, but he protected it well and burned me with a spin move. He laid the ball in the basket and they went up two with a minute and a half left.

I walked the ball up the court on the next possession. It was the biggest possession of the game and I didn't want to rush it. Our guys were dead tired though, and there was no movement. I had to make something happen myself. I called for a double-screen from both of our forwards. Mercy defended the first screen well, but the second one caught them off guard. It left me wide open for an elbow three—my favorite spot on the whole court. I stepped into it and knocked it down clean. The shot was in such rhythm, it felt so good leaving my hand—it didn't even touch the rim. All you heard was that sweet sound: *swish*.

Mercy called their final timeout. Our fans clapped and stamped their feet throughout. It was all about instincts now. Thoughts were useless.

I looked up to the stands and finally found my parents within the madness. They were clapping in unison with the rest of the crowd, swept up in all the frenzied emotion.

It was time to finish the game. It was time to become a part of Detroit's history. Neither team had a timeout left. Only overtime could extend the game. But I don't think either team wanted that. Nobody—coaches, players, even the fans—had the legs nor the stomach for another period. It was just too much.

Mercy inbounded the ball and dribbled up court. They dumped it inside to their power forward, who'd worn us out with twenty-nine points. This time, though, we were ready with a perfectly timed double-team. It was one of the double-teams that Coach drilled us on before the game. It was also one of the double-teams I went over with Dorrell after dinner.

We came up with a steal. That gave us the ball, up by one, with a minute left. I tried to waste some seconds off the clock, but they came with an aggressive trap. I passed to an open teammate, but he was nervous and didn't want the ball in that moment. I quickly went over to get the ball back from him in the front court. The clock wound down to forty seconds. For some reason, Mercy didn't bring another trap. Instead of playing it safe, I drove into the lane. There was a small crease in the defense and I was going to exploit it. I went up for a sweeping, left-handed layup and their power forward hit me on the wrist. The ref blew the whistle and the shot almost went in, but didn't. It was inches away from a three point play and a chance to put us up by four with thirty seconds left, essentially ending the game. Instead, I'd be on the free throw line.

The foul knocked their best player out of the game. They had to replace him with a player that hadn't played one minute. I went to the line and hit the first free throw. We were up by two. Hitting the second one would put us up three and pretty much ensure that we couldn't lose the lead in regulation.

I put the second shot up and it bounced in and out. Mercy rebounded the ball and quickly came the other way. I picked up the point guard on defense, right above the three point line. I anticipated him taking me down low again, but it never happened. Instead, he dumped the ball inside to the player they had just put in the game. Late in games, it was always our strategy to play defense straight up. Switch all screens. No double-teams—absolutely no double-teams. Especially, no double-teams on a player who was just coming into the game, ice cold.

For some reason, I peeled off my man and doubled the new player who had the ball down low anyway. This left my man open at the three point line. The player down low wasn't even in a good position to score. I don't know why I went down for the trap.

The player down low kept the ball high, away

from my swipes, and then kicked it back to the player who I was supposed to be guarding. My man drilled a wide open three and put them up by one with ten seconds to play.

The gym fell silent. That basket was on me.

The crowd was shocked. Coach's hands were on top of his head and his mouth was wide open. He could not believe his freshman star made a bone-headed play like that. With no timeouts left and no time to think—I took the inbound pass and rushed the ball into the front court. The scene was set up perfectly for me to go from goat to hero. Even with the great game, I'd only be remembered for the late mistake if we lost.

There were five seconds left. I hastily called for a couple of screens. I got loose on the second one once again. I dribbled to my spot at the elbow—right below the three point line this time—and elevated. I released the shot right as the buzzer sounded. The ball hung in the air for what seemed like thirty seconds.

It looked good. Right on-line and I was sure that it had enough arc. Everything was silent. Everyone's eyes were on the rock as it floated through the air.

It bounced in and out.

Game over. We'd lost to Mercy by one.

The sounds came back in the gym. They were muted, but there. Our crowd groaned. The patches of their crowd rejoiced. Mercy's bench players rushed the floor in celebration. My guys hit the deck, with their faces on the hardwood, trying to hide the tears.

I was frozen, taking it all in. After what seemed like ten minutes, I walked over to coach, who was still standing near the bench. We stood side-by-side, watching Mercy's players hugging one another. Their celebration at the center of our court was not disrespectful at all. We would've done the same if the outcome and venues were flipped.

The only sounds you could hear now, while our crowd filed out, came from Mercy. Their players were still celebrating and their cheering section sang their fight song at the top of their lungs.

A strange feeling came over me. It was bittersweet. I was sad that we lost, devastated that my bad defensive switch was the reason we lost. Still, a weird feeling of satisfaction was somewhere in there too. I forced a smile at Coach and he smiled back. He patted me on the head and told me that he loved me. He left the floor and all of my teammates did too. I just stood out there for a while longer, taking it all in.

Basketball, like life, can be a cruel thing. Sometimes life can be beautiful like a perfect swish. But it can also be a brick. And when you get a moment like that—like Mercy's players had on our home floor—you better relish it.

After finishing their celebration, all of the players plus the coaches from Mercy came over to congratulate us on a great game. I was gracious in defeat and felt proud of that. There was no sense in being bitter.

I finally went into the locker room. As expected, it was subdued. No words were spoken. Most of the guys were already changed by the time I got back there. I sat down in front of my locker and one by one, all of my teammates patted me on the shoulder as they left. Dorrell was the last one to stop by. I stood up and we looked each other in the eye. He gave me a dap along with a half-hug. I sat back down in front of my locker and just stared into it for a while. My hip was throbbing and my ears were ringing. I had proved myself tonight. We didn't win—but I had won over my teammates.

I showered slowly and changed clothes even more slowly. I walked gingerly out of the locker room and back into the gym. My parents were waiting there for me at mid-court. When I got to them, my mom rubbed my face and gave me a big hug. My dad put his arm around me and we shared a moment as a family again. That felt good. Being together like that gave me hope. Not that things would go back to how they used to be, but that we could be *something else.* Something different—but together in some way.

Neither of my parents said anything as we walked together to the parking lot.

We got to the two cars that were headed back to Auburn Hills. I would ride back in my mom's car and we'd head to the house that the three of us had shared for so many years. The place where the roots were supposed to be strongest. My father, on the other hand, would ride back to Auburn Hills in his black Mercedes. He would ride to some strange place, with strange people in it. Deep down, I knew that at some point, these people would be a part of my life. But not tonight.

Dad said a quiet goodbye to me and pulled me in close for a hug. He whispered in my ear that he was proud of me and that he loved me.

He got into his car and pulled away.

My mom and I got into her car and when my butt hit the seat, that's when it all hit me. We left school and drove north to Auburn Hills. We drove to our home. I said goodbye to Detroit once again and looked forward to the next hello. I did not feel ashamed for falling short of all my goals.

There was plenty more time.